Threads Unravel

Book Three of the Calypto Cycle

The Calypto Cycle

Fire in the Snow
Shackles of Doubt
Threads Unravel
Messages from the Sand (forthcoming in 2018)

Threads Unravel

D. Thomas Minton

Copyright © 2018 D. Thomas Minton
Cover art by Hans Binder Knott © 2018
Cover design by Holly Heisey

This book is available in print and electronic formats and at most online retailers.

ISBN: 0998304263
ISBN-13: 978-0-9983042-6-7

This one is for John and Gonny

PART I

SHIFTING SANDS

In winter, the Empire's central plain is hypnotic—flat land that seems to climb right up into the sky because the blowing snow obscures the horizon. I should have stayed in Zhadovka another night, but the woman at the guest house had said a storm was coming—she could feel it in her swollen knuckles—and if I didn't want to get stuck there until the melt, I had best try to outrun it. A poor choice, I realize now as I wipe at my stinging eyes, barely able to see the road through the snow glare.

I mumble a curse against R. She sent me here, wanting me to find a place safe from the trouble that hunts me, but I do not think such a place exists anymore.

Not after Coruşu.

Not after the betrayal, which hurts more than the scars on my wrists, still pink and tender, a testament to the brutality life—and Krauss—has delivered upon me.

I jolt awake again as a flash of red materializes in the road before me. I jerk the wheel and skid across the packed ice and drifting snow, sliding into the frozen grass before shuddering to a stop hard enough that I bang my head on the steering wheel.

My breaths come in rapid bursts. Had that been something actually in the road or a snow hallucination?

The handle of my FP is body-warm as I draw the pistol from its holster under my right arm. In the same motion, I turn, looking out the narrow back window rimed with ice. Several meters back another vehicle sits on the edge of the road. A woman stands next to it, her red scarf snapping in the wind like a pennant.

So, it wasn't a hallucination. A coincidence, then, that she's on the road at this time? It certainly could be, but in my business, things that look like coincidences can, in reality, be something much deadlier. I should just drive away; I don't think my auto has been damaged any more than my forehead, but what if this is exactly what it appears to be: a woman stranded in the snow? To leave her on the side of this desolate road is as good as putting a burst of fletchettes into her neck.

She has made no move to come toward me, likely because only seconds have passed since I nearly ran her down. I sense nothing wrong, nothing...out of alignment. I have a Talent for such things. Since I was small boy, I've had an uncanny awareness of imminent danger. When it's near, the world seems to slow down for a moment, and in those elongated seconds I find there is time for me to cheat fate. It has saved my life more times than I can count. Yet, like all Talents, mine has its limitations, and I cannot afford to be careless because they are searching for me. Who *they* are I don't know for certain, but a week ago I shook two men in heavy coats by slipping out a guest house window after the owner's warning. They could have been Red Cuffs or Silver Tigers, or even—and this one hurts the most to admit—aligned with The Order.

The woman in the red scarf starts toward me, approaching my auto's rear driver-side quarter.

I can't bring myself to drive away, so I set the brake. I slide across the bench seat and out the passenger door so that the auto is between us. The grass crunches under my shoes. Wind whips my hair. I haven't cut it in months, and I have taken to twisting it into short locs while I lie in bed at night, unable to settle my mind enough to sleep. I keep my FP lowered, but ready. My long coat and the auto block it from the woman's sight.

I scan the icy road and the frozen fields that dissolve into the blowing snow. If she is something other than stranded, she is either working alone or her partner is hiding in her vehicle, because there is nothing else out here.

"Are you okay?" she yells at me. I barely hear her over the wind.

"I didn't see you until the last minute," I say. She has her arms wrapped around herself so that I cannot clearly see her hands. Her red scarf is iced with a crust of snow, except where her warm breath has melted it.

"I was afraid I would miss anyone who came along."

That makes sense. I haven't seen a single auto since leaving Zhadovka four hours ago, and if experience is any indication, I won't see another all day. No one with any sense would be out here in this weather.

She has halted her approach, which allows me to keep both her and her auto in my sightline simultaneously.

"A bad day to be on the road," I say.

"I was bringing borscht to a sick friend." She doesn't carry herself like a threat, but looks are often deceiving. Her face is slender, and even in her bulky coat, I can tell she is not a large woman. In all her winter gear, I doubt she weighs fifty kilos.

"Your husband—"

"I don't have one. Not anymore."

She doesn't need to say anything else. The war with the Papalate has claimed many of the Empire's sons and brothers, fathers and husbands.

"Maybe I can help." I come forward cautiously, shifting my pistol so it is hidden behind my back. Her arms squeeze more tightly around her torso. If she is armed, it would be with a small, limited-shot pistol, but in the right hands, that is deadly enough.

She retreats to her auto, an older model that has seen better days. The body is dented and bruised with patches of rust. Based on the thickness of the snow on the windshield, she's been here an hour or more. The hood panels on either side are folded back.

She motions toward the exposed engine with a gloved, but otherwise empty hand.

I relax some, but I don't allow myself to get complacent. I circle around behind her and come up on her right side. As I do so, I glance into the cab of the auto. It is empty, and I get a good enough look to know whether anyone is in there. All the prints in the snow appear to match her small boots.

"It's spinning, but..." She shakes her head.

"Let me have a look." Keeping my weapon hidden, I walk around the front of the auto to the passenger side. There are no footprints in the snow over here, and I'm now more convinced that she is what she appears to be: stranded and in need of help.

"Thank you, Mister..."

"Titov," I say, giving her one of the alias I have been using the past few weeks. "Ivan Titov." The name still sticks to my tongue, and I am not sure I will continue to use it, but I feel I can no longer us Alexander Petrenko, because I am no longer that person. I need to find something new, something that suits my new reality.

I know almost nothing about engines, but slipping my FP into the pocket of my long coat, I poke my head under the hood panel, and ask her to engage the flywheel. The hum of the spinning wheel doesn't change. The engine makes an unsatisfying clicking noise, but the drive train does not engage. This is as much as I'm able to decipher, even if I'm not willing to admit it yet.

I come back around to the driver's side, and tug a few cables to check their connections, but to be honest I have no idea what any of them do. None of my actions affects the pitch of the flywheel.

A pair of lights emerges from the snow behind us and another auto rolls out of the whiteout. It comes up along the side and stops. The windshield is fogged over on the inside, edged with frost on the outside. The passenger door opens.

"Oh look, someone else to help." The woman leans out the window and waves her hand.

My spine tingles as the world around me shifts and stutters fitfully, like the gears of a pocket watch bent out of alignment. For a fraction of a second, the entire world freezes. The woman's frozen breath floats in a wreath around her head. Every snowflake hangs in the air as if suspended in a spider's web.

I throw myself over the auto's headlamps. As I tumble to the frozen ground, the world lurches forward again, as if whatever stone was lodged in the gears of time pops free. I scrabble against the front bumper as fletchettes ricochet off the hood and whistle over my head.

The woman's scream is cut off abruptly.

I fumble my weapon free of my long coat pocket.

She's dead, my brain screams, and my thoughts are a clatter of disjointed fears. Two men in dark coats...the same two from the guest house, but how did they find me again? None of these questions are important at the moment. These men are here, and they want to kill me.

I crawl around to the passenger side, putting the auto between me and my assailants, and scutter toward the rear of the auto, moving as quickly as I can on my hands and knees.

"Come out, come out," one of my assailants taunts me. His accent betrays an upbringing in one of the eastern provinces.

I slip around the back of the auto as he rounds the hood. I get to my feet as the second man comes around from the driver's side. Before I can react, he knocks my pistol away with a cudgel. The blow nearly breaks my hand and leaves me gasping for air. His next swing cracks against my skull and my vision goes white for a second. When it clears, I'm on my hands and knees, staring down at red blood drops in the snow.

"Don't kill him yet," the first one says. "We may need him still."

The one with cudgel grabs the collar of my coat and drags me roughly up the road. I pass the driver-side door. Blood runs down its side, dripping into a thickening puddle in the snow the size of a boot print.

My stomach wrenches. She's dead because of me. Guilty of nothing but hailing me down, and I thought I could help her. Now...

My throat is so tight I can barely breathe. This is what will happen to everyone who gets close to me. This is why I will never be able to do what R has ordered.

Then the blood and the auto are lost in the white curtain behind me, and I'm shoved hard to ground near my own vehicle.

"If he moves, shoot him," the man with the cudgel says.

I get a boot in my ribs, then make a sound worse than the blow warrants.

The one with the cudgel begins to search my auto, starting in the front.

The cut above my left eye bleeds freely, but other than momentarily stunning me, I don't think it's done any serious damage. Already my thoughts are clearing, allowing me to analyze my situation.

The man with the pistol stands behind me. His left boot is dark against the snowy backdrop. I suspect he has his pistol pointed at my back, ready to shoot. Carefully I raise my head so I can see my other assailant. He leans inside the auto, searching the front seat. Finding nothing, he moves to the back. He puts the cudgel on the rear seat as he bends further to look in the space under the front bench.

I fake a groan.

"It's cold out here," the one with the pistol says. He stamps his feet, trying to generate some heat. "Check the boot."

"You sure it's not on him?"

"Yes. Check the boot!"

My hands are nearly frozen, but I barely notice. I don't have my gloves or my hat.

The man comes out from the back of the auto and glares at his partner. He has a scar to the right of his chin that carves a notch in his otherwise full beard. He looks too disheveled to be a typical Red Cuff, but I cannot be certain.

He won't find what he's looking for in the boot because I no longer have the Celestial Orb. I buried it beneath a hedgerow outside of Kologriv. I could find it again if I need it, but it isn't the orb that is important. It's the phial of sand that was hidden inside, but that is buttoned safely in my shirt pocket, and it never leaves my person.

The man opens the boot, and I notice now that he has left his cudgel on the back seat.

The feet behind me shift closer to the back of the auto. The one with the pistol has gotten sufficiently cold that he's now distracted. "Hurry up. It's colder than the taxman's heart."

With as much force as I can generate, I strike back with my foot into the man's knee. I catch it squarely. He screams as his leg buckles, and I roll onto my back and swing my foot, catching his jaw with a sweeping kick that cracks several of his teeth. He is unconscious before he hits the ground.

I scramble for his pistol, getting it before the one with his head in the boot realizes what has happened.

I fire, but the weapon is unfamiliar and my fingers numb nearly to the point of being useless. The fletchettes whistle past him.

Instead of surrendering, the man scuttles behind the auto for cover. I get to my feet, and my head spins, causing me to stumble. I blink away the momentary vertigo and search for my assailant. Perhaps that blow to my head did more damage than I thought. I swing out wide from the vehicle and circle around the rear. He's not on the driver's side. I cautiously move forward, my gaze leaping over the area trying to see everywhere at once. He could have circled around the front or crawled underneath or—

I stop at a line of fresh footprints that lead out away from the auto into the fields. I can see nothing out there except blowing snow. I circle around the rest of the auto to make sure it's not a trick. Cautiously, I peer underneath and find nothing. By now, I cannot feel my finger on the pistol's trigger; I doubt I could shoot the weapon effectively. I take the cudgel from the backseat and tuck it into my belt.

My other assailant lies unmoving in the road. Snow collects on his back. He will freeze to death quickly, but I don't care.

I pull down the collar of his coat, expecting to find a tattoo on the back of his neck, but nothing is there. The Silver Tigers all seem to carry a mark—an inverted vee with a horizontal line inside of it and two more lines connected to form a right angle beneath it. Most often it has been on the neck, but I've also seen it on fingers, too.

I don't have the time, and it is too cold to conduct an exhaustive search. With a grunt, I flip him onto his back. I can't work the buttons on his coat, so I pat down his pockets. I find no billfold or other identification, but in his trousers pocket is a folded wad of bills, held closed with a money clip. No identification makes me believe even more that he is a Silver Tiger; a Red Cuff would carry his official papers.

I stuff the money into my long coat pocket. If nothing else, he owes me a nice dinner.

To be certain, I check on the woman and confirm that she is dead, the side of her face and throat perforated by shots never meant for her. I gently ease her back into the seat. A pang of regret stabs me at the thought of leaving her behind. She deserves more than to be left on the road alongside her murderer, but there is nothing I can do for her, and I cannot accommodate the trouble her dead body would cause me.

My throat hurts. "I'm sorry," I whisper, closing her open eyes. Her skin is already cold and ashen.

It isn't prudent to spend more time here. My missing assailant must soon return or risk freezing to death, and I don't want to be here when that happens. Desperate men are dangerous men. I put flechettes into the tires of my assailants' auto and also into the woman's for good measure. Then I shatter the windows with the cudgel. Let's see either of them survive the day now.

I check the back seat of my own auto through the rear window. It's as empty as I left it, so I latch the boot and climb behind the wheel. I blow warm air onto my hands and shove them into my gloves. My fingers ache as I work the blood back into them. I engage the drive, and it takes a few tries to work the vehicle back onto the road, but once on the pavement, the traction is good enough for me to get moving again. The other vehicles quickly fade into the whiteout behind me. With the rate snow is now falling, it might be spring before anyone finds them.

As I drive, I'm troubled by what has transpired. How did they find me again after I slipped away from them? Perhaps the proprietor of one of the inns at which I stopped was an informant, and recognized me. The Red Cuffs have many such ears spread throughout the Empire, and I encountered something similar with the Silver Tigers once in St. Stephensburg. I can't recall anyone who had acted strangely during the past few days, but a professional wouldn't do anything to raise suspicion. It's also possible the two had been zig-zagging every road day and night until they found my trail again. Most towns out here have only a single road running through them, so tracking me once they had my scent would not have been difficult.

The two also seemed to know exactly what they were looking for, but that doesn't allow me to confirm anything. While the Silver Tigers were the original owners of the Celestial Orb, the Red Cuffs also knew about it, but in Coruşu, they didn't seem overly interested in it, except as a means to pin treason on me.

I slap the steering wheel in frustration.

Whoever those two worked for—and there are several possibilities—knows my general location. I had hoped I had gotten away cleanly, but obviously that is not the case. This makes it clear that it is only a matter of time before the next pair of killers finds me. And I might not be so lucky next time. Not to mention anyone else who happens to be near me.

So, what is the use of being out here?

If I can't disappear in the frozen vastness of the Empire's central plains, then no place is safe. If I can't escape the fight, then I need to take the fight to them. To do that, however, I first need answers, and that starts with the phial of sand in my pocket. I don't know exactly who can answer my questions—to be honest, I don't even know what the questions are— but I have a good idea where to start.

Back where all this began.

Instead of dinner, I will use my assailant's cash for a ticket to Aurestapol. Before I do that, however, I need to make another stop. I have an advertisement to place in the Sunday *Gazeta* for an antique lamp.

THE TRAIN WHEELS CLACK and squeal as we switch tracks and make a wide eastward arc before plunging into the darkness of Aurestapol's underground tunnels. The lamps in the carriage corridor flicker several times before deciding to stay on. The light bleeds past the edges of the shade on my compartment door, splattering in a knife-line across the floor. Outside, tunnel supports flash by in the near dark, ticking off the distance. Occasionally a red light blurs into a line across the blackness like a comet's fiery tail.

I reach above my head and pull the cord on the compartment's reading lamp. It throws a meager halo of light onto the small, stoppered phial in my hand. As I shift the cylinder, the sand within flows from one end to the other like talc.

My thoughts are drawn to the lives this phial has taken. The nameless woman on the road is just the latest.

Carlos was killed by Krauss as he helped me escape the Red Cuff prison. If Carlos hadn't sprung me, I would have died there, I have no doubts about that now. While Krauss hadn't broken me to the point of confessing to something I hadn't done, he *had* broken me, and if Carlos had not been there to force me to act, it was only matter of time before Krauss finished me. For that, I will always be in Carlos's debt.

Dai Li is also likely dead, shot down in the tunnels beneath Coruşu by Krauss and his Red Cuff thugs.

Catherine and Arkady Petrescu's status likely insulated them from harm, but consequences don't have to be fatal to be consequential. I've never heard what happened to them; news of their fate never penetrated the snowy central plains.

These are the ones of which I know. There may be others.

I shake my head.

Sand. What secrets does it hide among its grains?

I'm sure it hides something. It had been a message meant for the Silver Tigers—that much I know—but a message about what?

At night, while lying in strange beds in strange towns in the middle of nowhere, I would stare at the sand well into the darkest hours. I discerned nothing from looking at it however, either in the yellows glare of the bedside lamp or the blue glow of the moon or if I poured it out a saucer and spread the grains thinly across the porcelain surface. Neither did its odor, its taste, or its gritty feel between my fingers reveal anything about its secret.

So, to Aurestapol I come.

If anyone can help me, I will find that person here.

The darkness falls away suddenly as the train emerges from the tunnel into Aurestapol's Grand Station. With a final pop of the brakes, we shudder to a stop at an empty platform. The compartment's lamp flickers twice and goes out as the engineer powers down the train.

I tuck the glass phial into my shirt pocket, and check my watch. Twenty-one past the hour and right on time. The watch slides back into my trouser pocket, weighting the bottom like ballast. I shrug on my long coat and retrieve the battered fedora I acquired in Coruşu. The black bloodstain on the underside of the brim is a reminder of my time on the Romani plateau. I perch the hat on my head as I study the platform out the carriage window.

Passengers trickle off the train, but otherwise the platform is oddly empty. I'm not sure what I expected, but part of me thought I would find a line of Red Cuffs waiting for me. I wouldn't put it past Krauss to know exactly what train I was on.

I wait in my compartment until the platform and stairs up to the station's lobby are more crowded before taking my leave. The platform is chilly and smells sharply of coal smoke, and I let the crowd carry me through a cloud of locomotive steam toward the exit. Up the stairs, the methodical thump of shoes echoes in the small space. At the top is a circle of light, and, reaching it, I pass through into the lobby. A dome vaults high overhead, and in the center of the vast space is a massive clock face that chimes half past the fifteen hour.

That was the same time I left this station a month ago.

Across from where I stand, uniformed men—likely newly commission officers—ring the café table where R gave me my ticket and my orders. From the grim expressions on their young faces, they await their military transport to the front. Throughout the bleakness of my exile, fresh news was hard to come by, and I realize now as I see the soldiers around me, that I have no idea of the current status of the war with the Papalate. I doubt anything has changed because nothing has changed in several years, especially during the winter, when the snows and mud bog down the strategy. For the past two years, the Westari front has been stagnant, shifting never more than a hundred meters one way or the other.

Yet, I feel that something could have changed, when I wasn't looking. In fact, something *must* have changed, or my experience in Coruşu will lose any meaning.

I slide forward through the shifting mass of people. The noise echoes indistinctly in the great lobby and the voices and the tapping of shoes on the tile and the clatter of the clapperboard all mix into a miasma of meaningless sound. Yet it is sound, rich and full and more alive than the lonely voices ripped away by the wind across the plains.

The war may have crippled many of the Empire's small hamlets and robbed its rural poor of comfort and hope, but Aurestapol is still alive, fed by the blood of nationalism. People here still have the means to travel, to live, and the Grand Station is the Empire's pulsing heart.

This offends me.

I cut across the lobby. Overhead the clapperboard cycles for the third time since my arrival—a cascade of tiles realigning as a half-dozen trains depart. I buy a copy of yesterday's Sunday *Gazeta*, and retreat to a spot along the wall where other smartly dressed travelers review today's broadsheet. I turn to the classifieds and scan down until I find it.

> For Sale. Orthodox Lampada.
> Bronze Enamel, St. Vladimir's
> cross. Circa 1830. Contact Osip.
> Box 3368

They got it right, a minor miracle considering the aptitude of the wire clerk in Chyobsara who helped me.

I hand the paper back the newsboy, who gives me a quizzical look, but I offer him no explanation as I turn away. The west exit spills me out onto the street with a dozen other people who snap up their collars and disperse in every direction. I lower my hat brim and lean into the wind as I turn north.

Away from the Grand Station, the crowd quickly thins. I double my pace; I must hurry if I'm going to get to the university before dusk. The Imperial Institute of Science and Technology is on the west side of Korelov Park, at least a thirty-minute walk from the station.

Winter is far from over, but the air is unseasonably warm and the ice has melted, leaving only a few mounds of blackened snow pushed into the alleyways between the buildings. The cloud pack diffuses the light into a watery gray color. An old woman with scarves stacked to cover all but her weary eyes, glares at me as she splashes past. Her anger of loss is palpable. A son, a husband, a brother, a daughter— the gears of war do not care, and she glares at me as if I have dodged my civic duty through misanthropy or privilege or, worse, that I am one of the leaders responsible, however unlikely my shabby appearance makes that.

Then she is gone, and I am alone with the tenements, dreary gray walk-ups mottled black like moth wings with coal soot. Roots from gaunt, leafless trees push up the stones, turning the sidewalk into hazardous terrain. An occasional auto whirs past, infrequent enough to draw attention.

I turn onto a cross street and my steps falter as the tenements on the north side give way to Korelov Park. I have always thought the park to be beautiful, but today it has an aura of sadness. The boughs of the dark pines droop heavily, and in the slanting afternoon light, the colors are a rich palette of sorrow-muted greens and browns.

That night—how many months ago now? I had carried Lera down this street after she had nearly destroyed herself to save me. Even with my wounds, she had felt insubstantial in my arms, like a feather from a dove that would be whisked away on the slightest breath. That was the last time I saw Lera, or at least have memory of seeing her. According to R, she and Birdie were the ones who found me in Coruşu, frozen to within minutes of death. That's twice for which I now owe Lera.

I follow the perimeter of the park as it curves north again until I come to Aurestapol's great library. Two blocks west of the library, I come to a simple set of stone obelisks that marks the edge of the university campus. The cobblestone streets and dingy brick buildings give way to tree-lined lawns, covered with a skin of decaying leaves. The gravel paths wind between white stone buildings, most of which date back a century or more, to when artisans took pride in the sweeping lines of their arches and the majesty of their neoclassical domes and leaded-glass windows.

Years ago, Odella and I would come down here and pretend we were carefree students by laying on a blanket near one of the fountains or a bed of roses. Neither of us had attended university—we weren't "university material"—but the campus was serene and beautiful, and the students had a life and vigor about them that stood in stark contrast to the world in which we lived. That was before the hostilities with the Papalate erupted into full-out war. Before everything went wrong with Odella.

Prior to my recent mission to Olesk, I had not seen Odella since the disastrous end to our relationship, but fate brought me to her doorstep, and I learned that she—that we—had a daughter. Odella had hidden Maya from me. In truth, she had erased me entirely from the girl's world by not even telling her who I was. Rationally, I know Maya is better off not knowing. I am in no position to be a good father—I don't even know what a good father is because I never had one—but that doesn't mean I couldn't have become a good one. We are not pre-determined to follow a single path through life. While I have accepted that I cannot change the past, I possess free will to shape that which is yet to come.

I shake away the thoughts of Odella and my daughter. Right now I couldn't be a father even if I had the opportunity, and I may not even be alive tomorrow. More importantly, Maya is safer if she stays far away from me, and if no one every finds out her true identity, because I do not know the lengths my enemies will go to get to me.

I ARRIVE AT MY DESTINATION as the cloud-muted sun settles atop the trees. It must be just past the top of the hour because a crowd of young men filters from a lecture hall and congregates in the atrium of the science building. I haven't seen this many young men out of uniform in one place since the conflict with the Papalate escalated. Their crisp shirts and ties, starched trousers and dark coats betray their privilege. These are not boys who will be shipped to the front to become fodder for the beast; instead they will find their way to remote outposts or into the command tents far behind the trenches and blood-soaked no man's land.

I skirt the edge of the crowd to a faculty directory board, but the dozen or so names are meaningless to me because no specialties are listed, only office numbers. I rub at the stubble peppering my chin; the prospect of going office to office holds little appeal.

"You look like you could use some help," a man with a gray beard says. In the din of the conversations I hadn't heard him come up alongside me. He wears a

21

suit coat several sizes too small for his round belly, and his hands are stuffed into his trouser pockets. "You don't exactly look like one of my students," he says when I don't immediately respond.

My first reaction is to turn him away because I'm suspicious of his motives, but he is likely nothing more than what he appears. "I'm not a student," I say, allowing a smile to warm my features. "You are right; I could use some help."

"I am Professor Voynov." The ink-stained cuffs of his shirt peek out from his coat sleeve as he extends his hand. His grip is unexpectedly strong. "How can I help you?"

I resist an urge to lean close to him and whisper my request. "I am looking for someone who can tell me something about some sand I have."

The professor's bushy eyebrows pinch together. "Sand, you say? Hmm. What sort of *something* were you hoping to learn?"

"I don't know exactly," I say, purposely being evasive.

"I'm an agronomist," he says. "I study soils and plants," he explains when I don't respond. "My specialty is farm productivity, so I know fair bit about dirt, as I like to say." His eyes twinkle, and it's obvious that his passion is genuine, even if his joke is stale. "Soil is a bit different from sand, but I might be able to help."

"I would appreciate that. Is there somewhere...quieter we can talk?"

"Of course. My office is..." He turns into the crowd and his voice is swallowed in the noise. The students part before him, and I follow in the professor's wake. He leads me into a hallway that

runs down one wing of the building. Unlike the
atrium which is spacious and well lit by an antique
chandelier, the hallway is shadowy and cluttered with
boxes and dusty display cases stocked with jars,
chunks of rock, and the skulls of exotic animals.
Tucked in among the clutter are narrow doors with
panes of beveled glass that lead into what I assume
are faculty offices. Most of the windows are dark, but
a few are lit, and from one comes the clacking of a
typewriter.

At the end of the hallway, Professor Voynov
opens the last door and motions me into an office
lined with shelves tightly packed with books and
loose papers. Taking up the majority of the limited
floor space is Voynov's prodigious desk, cluttered
with typewritten papers, folders, books, and a half-
eaten sandwich that could be several days old,
considering the stale-looking crust. Behind the desk is
a doorway covered with a grayed sheet tacked to the
frame.

Voynov clears away a stack of books from a hard-
backed chair and motions for me to sit. His own chair
squeaks in protest as he settles behind the desk.

"Now please, Mister..."

"Titov," I say, still determined to give this alias a
try.

"Please, Mr. Titov, tell me how I might assist you."

I reach inside my coat, but stop. The sounds of
conversation echo down the hallway from the atrium.
To be honest, they aren't so loud as to bother me, but
I close the door anyway. "You don't mind, do you?"

"No, no. That's quite okay."

I sit again, and this time remove the phial from its
place inside my shirt pocket. "I want to learn more

about this sand," I say.

"May I?"

Hesitantly I place the phial into the professor's extended hand. This is the first time since obtaining it I've let it out of my possession, and I find it difficult to let it go even if it's to a man who presents no threat to me and might be able to illuminate its secrets.

Voynov holds the phial up to the dingy overhead light. "What is it you would like to know?"

"To start, where it came from."

Voynov squints at me over the cork stopper. "That's what I was going to ask you," he says. Unsatisfied with the ceiling light, he pulls the cord on his desk lamp and thrusts the phial into the halo of light. The sand tumbles inside as he slowly rotates the cylinder. "It looks marine," he says.

"You mean like beach sand?"

"It could be dredge too, I suppose. Look how white it is," Voynov says. "I think it's calcium carbonate, like the stuff in snail shells—definitely not from any lake or river around here. That would be more brown."

"Can you tell me where it's from?"

"Sand is quite a bit different from soil, so I'm not sure how much I can help you."

"But theoretically it's possible?"

"If this was soil, I could probably narrow it down based on grain size, organic material and mineral composition, but sand like this is a little different. It's all mostly the same mineral, but one thing I do know is this white stuff usually comes from warm seas. Would you mind if I looked at it more closely?"

I nod permission, and Voynov removes a small

glass dish out of a desk drawer and carefully pours the sand into it. He excavates a magnifying glass from under a stack of papers and trains it on the dish. "Yes, definitely warm seas," Voynov says. He hands me the magnifying glass and gestures toward the dish of sand.

I lean over and move the magnifying glass towards and away from my face, adjusting the focal length until the sand grains come it focus.

Who ever thinks about sand? It's the stuff one walks on at the beach—just ground-up rock, like dirt. Yet under the magnifying glass, what I see makes me pull back in surprise. Chunks of rock in various colors, some translucent like miniature pieces of broken glass, but most of the sand is small, white opalescent shells, no bigger than a pinhead but fully formed like a snail shell I might hold in my hand. Mixed among these different shell types are small, star-like white objects, little white spheres, and white disks, all peppered with systematic grids of small holes. Thousands of these tiny organisms in only a half teaspoon of sand!

"Amazing, yes?" Voynov asks.

Amazing is too mild a word. "I've never seen anything like it."

"Nearly everything in there is the shell of an animal of some kind," Voynov explains. "Snails, foraminifera, bits of stuff from bigger things. I suppose if one of those creatures has a limited distribution, you might could narrow down the origin of the sand, the same way we could narrow the location of a soil sample if it had a rare mineral in it."

"Who could do that?"

Voynov's chair squeaks as he settles back into it.

He rubs his gray beard and stares off past me. "Hmmm... Dr. Arif Özel is a professor at the Science and Technical University at Çavuş in the Sultanate who studies beach-forming processes. He might be able to help. If nothing else, he knows more people than I do in that particular field. This could take a long time, though; communications with the Sultanate aren't what they used to be."

I concede this point. Rumors have been swirling for months that the Sultanate is already violating its declaration of neutrality and aiding our enemy. Rumors are not always true, however, and the lack of response shows at least the Empire's uncertainty in these allegations. Regardless of the truth, the relationship between our nations is strained beyond anything conducive to cooperation, let alone friendship, and even though the lines of communication with the Sultanate are still open and theoretically possible, communiques have slowed to a crawl.

"I don't have the luxury of time," I say. "Is there another way? Perhaps someone locally?"

Voynov steeples his fingers against his chin as he thinks. "Science, like women, can't be rushed if you wish to succeed, Mr. Titov." The corners of his mouth turn up slightly at his joke. "Let me call on a colleague in another department. He is a biologist who has spent some time in the tropics. He might know something about those little creatures in the sand. Unfortunately, it's a bit late today to catch him, but I can find him tomorrow morning. Would you mind if I held onto this sample in case he is able to look at it? I assure you it will be safe with me."

He must have sensed my reluctance because he

said the last part in a tone much like a parent might use to cajole a favorite toy from a toddler at bedtime. I should be offended, but honestly, I am more hesitant than any reluctant toddler to let that phial out of my sight. If anything were to happen to it, I would lose the only clue I have. I believe I can trust Voynov, however; he seems to be an honest academician. That is not the issue. The matter is more who might come looking for it. The professor does not look capable of defending himself, let alone the sand. As much as I would not want to lose the phial, I also wish to see no harm come to Voynov. People have already died, and I suspect others still will before this is over.

To my knowledge, however, no one knows I am in Aurestapol, so perhaps my concern is misplaced. I do not intend to be here long enough for Krauss or Katalin Kovac or the Silver Tigers to learn of my whereabouts, so the risk to Voynov's safety appears to be low. Finally, I don't know where else to turn, and without help, that sand is essentially worthless to me.

After what seems like a very long pause, I say, "You can hold on to it."

Voynov gives me a curt, serious nod meant, I am certain again, to reassure me.

"Shall I call again tomorrow afternoon?" I ask.

"If you have access to a telephone, ring first, around fourteen o'clock. I might not have any news to share." He scribbles a telephone number on a scrap of paper and hands it to me across the desk. "That connects to Mrs. Sokolova in the department office. I will leave a message with her about whether a visit would be worth your time."

I take the slip of paper and tuck it into my pocket

without looking at it. I have no idea if I will be near enough to a telephone tomorrow afternoon to ring the department office, and frankly, I doubt it will matter. Whether he has had time to connect with his colleague or not, I will be paying the professor another visit. "It's no bother to come by," I say.

Voynov shrugs. "I'll see you tomorrow then, but if you change your mind, you know where to call."

I thank the professor and rise. As I turn to leave, I hesitate, unable to shake nagging concerns. What if something happens to my phial: dropped or misplaced or lost as the result of any number of increasingly implausible scenarios? I almost ask for the phial back, but don't, and I'm left standing awkwardly in the no man's space between Voynov's desk and the door.

Voynov watches me quizzically.

To cover my uncertainty, I ask, "What was the name of the gentleman in the Sultanate again?"

The corners of the professor's mouth lift slightly, as if he recognizes my poor attempt to cover my insecurities. Yet he says nothing, and instead tears off another scrap of paper from some poor student's report. He scribbles a name on it in messy script and hands it to me. "Dr. Arif Özel. If you bring him a good bottle of *raki*, he'll do just about anything for you."

Having spent some time in the Sultanate, I understand such sentiment. Good *raki* is worth a large favor.

I SNAP UP THE COLLAR of my long coat to ward off the chill and head back across campus. I have plenty of time to reach my next destination, but I walk quickly to stay warm. The temperature is dropping rapidly with the failing dusk, and it might become cold enough to snow tonight.

I take a circuitous route, watching for evidence I'm being followed, but the street behind me is always empty and the eyes of the passersby and loiterers always uninterested.

Only one person should know I'm in Aurestapol, but that's why I need to be cautious. Complacency is an operative's greatest danger.

My route takes me down by the Moskova, the river's black waters dimly lit by the wharves along the western bank. Many of the moorings are empty, the cargo ships that would have been there re-routed to ports closer to the front, but stevedores offload pallets from a handful of small vessels. Aurestapol is not a shipping center—the river is narrow and shoaled in many places. Proposed construction of a canal north to the Vlaga has been delayed because the men who would dig the ditches have been diverted to the fronts. I have heard that the Ministry of Transportation has asked to use prisoners of war to complete the canal, but no work has begun yet. Military ironsides now line the wharves, although I don't understand their benefit. The presence of military guns does nothing to enhance the defense of a city already deep behind the lines. There may be some morale benefit that I don't appreciate, but consistent coal supplies and fresh vegetables would likely do more than iron and powder.

By the time I cut away from the river's edge and back toward the city center, night has fallen entirely. Thick blackout curtains have ensured the buildings are shadowy blocks of darkness, but fortunately the moon is up, giving the clouds a faint glow under which it is sufficient for me to see.

I arrive at the steps of St. Vladimir's church at exactly eighteen-thirty.

"You're late." R steps out of the shadows at the top of the stairs. I can't see her well in the darkness, but I would know her tough, raspy voice anywhere.

"I'm not late," I say, slightly irked.

She takes my elbow and maneuvers me back into the shadows of the church entry, near the great wooden doors where we are invisible from the street. R is several inches shorter than me and thirty years older, I would guess, although age is slippery currency with R. I know her only in the capacity of being my handler, the person who gives me missions and berates me for being late or sloppy or whatever seems to offend her professional sensibilities on a particular day. It is easy to never think of her as someone who killed men with her bare hands if she needed—or wanted—but I'm sure she spent time in the field before becoming what she is now, and I have no doubts she was as efficient a field operative as she is a handler.

"I told you to disappear," R says. "You should not have come back. You put yourself and others in needless danger."

I want to tell her I'm safer here than out there. Who would suspect I would come back to Aurestapol? But I've learned to choose my arguments with R. "It's good to see you too," I say. "My message wasn't too cryptic?"

"You're not as clever as you think, or you would have gotten the day into your message along with the place and time. It was cold last night."

I look down at my shoes in the darkness. The critique stings, but I decide to push the conversation forward. "I haven't heard from you, and—"

R makes a dismissive sound and waggles her hand at me, as if to shoo away my concern.

"—I can't keep running."

I tell R what happened on the frozen highway outside of Zhadovka, my voice tightening painfully when I get to the woman. As I speak, I remember the way the woman's blood pooled and froze in the snow. "I don't know who they are or how they found me, but I'm not safer out there than I am here. There is nowhere to hide."

"When has it ever been safe for you?" R's tone carries no sympathy; it is as hard as the fact she voices.

Growing up a scrawny, self-aware child—different in so many ways—made me a magnet for the bullies who populated the state orphanages. My adult life has been no less peppered with dangers, with a continuous series of missions into dangerous territory. In all these cases, however, I knew generally the source of the threat, which gave me an advantage when dealing with it.

"That's not the point," I say. "I can't hide from this. It's too big."

R says nothing, and in the shadows, I can't see her face to gauge her thoughts. In the tense silence, I sense she is holding something from me.

"This all goes back to Coruşu," I say.

"Don't."

I exhale my frustration, my breath silvery in the faint moonlight. Every time I have tried to talk about Coruşu, she has shut me down, insisting the less she knows the better. I disagree because R has a broader perspective that could bring insight. The only reason for her not to know is she's concerned that someone will try to force the information from her.

"I was reassigned," R says. "Quite suddenly, too."

Unable to hide my surprise at this news, I stutter a half-formed thought that R ignores.

"Someone decided my talents were better used boxing meaningless files for movement to the archive. That means I was either close to something, or I was in a position that would allow me to get close to something."

In that moment R is speaking, I regain my wits. "That also means someone is on onto you."

"When are you going to learn to ask the right questions, Calypto?"

She's right, but this news generates so many potentially "right" questions, starting with: who moved her?

"I don't know who ordered it," R says, apparently reading my thoughts. "And no, I wasn't followed."

She says this right as the thought enters my head. Presumably, whoever reassigned her knows she was asking questions that they wanted left unanswered. By extension, they also have her under surveillance.

"I would expect nothing less," I say.

She grunts dismissively at my somewhat snide comment.

"What this does confirm are my suspicions about Coruşu," R says.

My stomach sours at the thought of betrayal. For several weeks, I had been reluctant to entertain this possibility simply because it couldn't be true. The Order rescued me from my previous life, and made me what I am. I have given my life to The Order, but denial can only carry one so far in the light of mounting evidence. While I had come to accept the possibility that some in The Order had turned on me, I continued to hold out slim hope that I was wrong. Now R has crushed that hope.

"It could be a small group of agents acting alone, but we must consider the possibility that everyone in The Order, unless we have solid reason to think otherwise, is involved." R's words lack emotion, as if even she finds them difficult to say. "But we must also accept that we do not know enough to judge motives or loyalty."

Motives and loyalty?

"They're trying to kill me." The words just blurt out, like a scream of pain when being stabbed in the back.

"Nothing is certain at this point."

Her words are meant to placate me, but they don't. "You believe this is some misunderstanding?" I ask.

"Get your head about you, Calypto, or someone *will* kill you."

R is right. She is always right.

I take several deep breaths, but they don't still my shaking hands.

"We don't know if this is a cabal or systemic," R says. "Likewise, we do not know their reasons or motives, and we must acknowledge the reality that we do not have all the information. Lacking that, we cannot know if any of this is justified."

R may be right that we don't know the motives of The Order, but that cannot justify betrayal or make it any less heinous or painful.

"These are things I am working on, and your presence here does nothing to aid that. You should not have come back, but what is done is done; time does not give us 'do-agains.'" She nudges my jaw with a gloved hand so I am looking at her. "We must look forward, yes?"

"Agreed."

"Good. Now some news, so this rendezvous is not an entire waste of my evening," she says. "I am getting close to something. I can feel it, even if I can't see what it is yet. Shh, let me finish. You are right that this is about Coruşu, but it is about more than that— much more than that. Coruşu was a result of something that goes much deeper and broader."

"Is this truth or conjecture?" I ask.

"Right now, some of both, but I believe it will prove to be all of one in due time. The gears of something have been put into motion, and Coruşu, I believe, was an attempt to stop it. I do not yet know what *it* is, but I will not stop until I do."

"That is why you were moved, to stop you from finding out."

"It will not stop me."

"Surely whoever moved you knows that, so why not just make you disappear?"

She doesn't answer me, and I imagine the expression on her face, the one I cannot see in the darkness but which chides me again for asking the wrong question. Then the right question comes to me and the answer seems obvious.

"Me?"

"I must still have some value," R says, "even if it is as a worm to your fish."

Whoever *they* are wants me, and they know my connection to R. It would take no significant leap of logic to surmise if I was going to contact anyone, it would be her, and they would be right.

"You need to get out of there," I say.

"Your concern is touching, but I'm fine."

"For how long?"

"That's not important. If I leave, I will learn nothing, and I suspect leaving would also not guarantee my safety."

"How long until you wind up dead?"

"Some things are bigger than me or you and any person. Besides, I am not careless and without friends."

"There are no friends in this business," I say, repeating a line she has told me many times. It was one of the first things taught to us in our initial training—an operative has no friends, nor room for them. True friends will be used against you, and any other kind of friend is really no friend at all. In this business, you trust only two people: your handler and yourself.

"True, so true," R says, "but it may be time for us to throw away the old rules because they are now the rules of our adversaries. Trust your instincts, Calypto."

"My instincts?"

But R isn't paying attention to me anymore. She has gotten more fidgety the longer our meeting has gone on. "I need to get back before I am missed."

"What?"

"I haven't been followed, but that doesn't mean I am not being watched."

I try to say something, but she cuts me off.

"That is not your concern right now. Your concern is getting out of Aurestapol. Whatever you learned in Coruşu is important, but I suspect it is not the only thing they seek."

While R knows nothing about the phial, her meaning is not lost. I believe Coruşu was as much about me as the phial of sand, and it is quite possible that while we are now together, we are not truly linked. The gears of my betrayal were set into motion long before the phial and I became intertwined. Yet, this still changes nothing.

"My business here isn't done."

R grunts her disapproval, but she does not ask me to elaborate. "I feared you would say something like that. You have already disobeyed me, so I doubt you'll listen this time."

"New rules," I say.

She presses a sharp metal object into my hand. A key. "Eleven Bogdanova Fare," she says. "Be discreet."

My left eyebrow slides up into an arch. She expected my disobedience. I should not be surprised anymore by anything R knows or does. I am glad I'm on her side.

I slip the key into the pocket of my long coat.

"We cannot meet again." R turns to leave, but hesitates. "Be careful, Calypto," she says. Then as quickly as she was there, she is gone down the church steps and into the gloom of the night.

Her departure leaves a palpable hole in the world around me. I don't want to accept it, but she is right; we cannot meet again. At least not until all this is over.

I WAIT A FULL FIVE MINUTES before slipping from the shadows of St. Vladimir's and into the dark of the night. I stick to small side streets to avoid any chance encounters with a local *mussor* patrol looking to chop-bust anyone whose appearance even hints they might be a rascal. I don't need more complications, not with what already feels like the entire world after me, and curfew is less than an hour away, so the lower my profile, the better.

I head toward Bogdanova Fare and R's safe house. I need to cross larger thoroughfares to get there, so I snap up the collar of my long coat and tilt down the brim of my hat to obscure my face. Leaning into the cold wind, I am nearly unidentifiable. Not that there is much of anyone out at this time of the night. Alone, I am left to my thoughts, which are not comforting, but try as I do, I cannot shake the implications of what R has confirmed. The Order is working against me. I don't know why, but things started to go wrong the morning I witnessed the assassination of Alexander Olstevski by the Silver

Tigers a kilometer from where I am now.

I'm so lost in my thoughts I don't immediately notice the shadow coming toward me. He must not have noticed me either in the dark. I see him at the last moment, his head also down against the cold, and I try to side-step him, but we clip shoulders, and I nearly knock him from his feet. I catch his elbow and save him from stumbling to the pavement.

"Pardon," the man says coolly, never looking at me and instead brusquely brushing aside my hand and continuing on his way.

My nose crinkles at the strong odor of tobacco left in the man's wake.

I glare at his back as he starts to sink into the night. I know I should ignore his rudeness; likely he is only trying to get home before curfew. Yet there is something oddly familiar about him. The timbre of his voice... I know it, and the smooth aroma of the tobacco. Not a cheap cigarette smell, but that of quality leaf that would need to be hand-rolled. I am taken back to Coruşu and a meeting beneath a bridge as military transports rumbled overhead. It smelled just like *that* tobacco.

Mélon.

I am nearly certain of it.

I should turn and continue on my way before he identifies me—who knows how he would react. That is what I should do, but which I don't. Instead I follow a half-block behind him, taking care to keep my footfalls light on the pavement and in time with his own.

I loosen my long coat and slip my hand inside to rest on the handle of my FP. It is warm and solid in my palm, one of the few tangible things in the unreality that my life has become. A deep breath calms my nerves and focuses my mind. I must be on my guard. As a member of The Order, Mélon is certain to have a Talent, but what that Talent may be is beyond my guess.

I keep Mélon at the edge of my vision. More than once, I think I will lose him the darkness, but a few quick strides and his shadowy form rematerializes.

Several minutes go by, and I'm wondering now why I am following him. This risk is foolish and dangerous. What if he realizes he is being followed, or worse, he recognizes me? Succeeding in Aurestapol requires I not be made by those who wish me harm. Worse, yet, what if this wasn't a chance encounter, but one staged to lead me into a trap? That seems unlikely. I have been very careful, yet... I shake my head and continue to follow. My instincts tell me that following Mélon is the right thing to do, so I continue to tail him through the dark streets until he suddenly comes to a stop and starts to look around.

I duck behind a stoop and watch him through the bars of the wrought iron railing. I don't think he saw me. He scans the street in every direction before ducking into a narrow alleyway. I count five, and when he doesn't reappear, I scuttle forward, staying as close to the tenements as I can. I edge up to the alleyway and press my back against the coal-dark stones of the building and peer around the corner. It's like staring into a well the alley is so dark, but Mélon is down there, his whispered voice just loud enough to be heard, but too soft for me to parse the words. Then a second, barely audible voice comes through the blackness.

I strain to see with whom he is meeting, but the

darkness is as impenetrable as ink.

He must have thought them to be unobserved because Mélon strikes a match and lights a cigarette. In that momentary flash of flame, I see clearly the face of his companion. Her delicate features look painted on her teardrop-shaped face, like that of a fine porcelain doll. But beneath that beauty is a calculating coldness that could freeze the warmest heart.

All my muscles go tense to the point of being painful.

Then, with a shake of the match, the light is gone, and the night collapses in on Mélon and Katalin Kovac.

For her sake, I prayed our paths would never cross again because of the harm I have dreamed about doing to her as payback for Coruşu and justice for Carlo. She allowed Krauss to do his will on me to break me and make me confess to crimes I would never consider committing.

But what else did I expect from a Red Cuff?

R's voice whispers to me from the recesses of my mind. I can't hear the words clearly, but I know what she's telling me—don't let my emotions overwhelm rational thought.

I force my grip to loosen on my FP and pull my hand from inside my long coat. The cold air sweeps in and freezes the sweat trickling down my sides, extracting a convulsive shiver from me. I retreat behind the corner of the building, holding my breath as I listen. Did they hear me?

No footsteps coming up the alley, and between gusts of wind, I hear Mélon's soft voice again.

After a few seconds, I peer once more into the

alleyway. When Mélon draws on his cigarette, the glowing tip casts just enough light that my night-acclimated eyes see both him and Katalin. Bathed in the red light, they have demonic casts upon them.

Why would Mélon be meeting with a Red Cuff? The Order and the Red Cuffs have never cooperated well, mostly a fault of the Red Cuffs who don't play well with anyone; it is not in their nature. They see spies and traitors everywhere, and it is their mission to root them out for the good of the Empire. No one, except the Emperor and maybe the Inspector General, are above their suspicion, and it would not surprise me if at some levels of the Red Cuffs, even they are not beyond reproach.

The cigarette tip flares again as Katalin hands Mélon an envelope. The next time it brightens the envelope is gone, and I assume Mélon has slipped it into his coat pocket.

I don't have time to ponder what she could have given him, however. Footsteps move toward me. I retreat quickly into the shadows near a stoop and freeze as Mélon steps from the alleyway. His cigarette tip glows red in the night as he scans the street before turning and walking past me, back the way he came.

Katalin doesn't come out of the ally, and I'm suddenly torn. Do I stay with her or follow Mélon? I fall in behind Mélon. My instincts tell me the contents of that envelope are more important than Katalin Kovac.

I follow him carefully for several blocks to put distance between us and his meeting place. Maybe Mélon doesn't know who Katalin Kovac is; she fooled me in Coruşu, so maybe she is playing Mélon, too. The only one who can answer that is Mélon, but how would he react to me? On which side do Mélon's loyalties lie? Not knowing, I must assume the worst.

I follow him for another block, placing my footsteps quietly so as not to tip him off. The wind is in my face, blowing away any soft sounds I may make. I slide my FP from its holster.

I quicken my pace.

The distance between us shrinks.

Mélon looks back at the sound of my footsteps. I don't try to soften them now, but walk hard and with purpose, as if I am an ordinary citizen hurrying to beat curfew home. Taking no chance, I lower my head so the brim of my hat obscures my face.

He slows to let me by.

As I draw up alongside of him I grab his arm and shove the tip of my pistol into the space between his bottom two ribs. "Keep walking, Mélon," I say, looking into his face. It may be dark, but this near to his nose I see him well enough as his eyes widen with recognition. For some reason, his expression gives me considerable satisfaction.

"Make any move near your weapon, and I'll shoot."

"Don't get jittery," Mélon says.

"Then don't make me that way."

We continue down the street. I keep close to him, my FP pressed into his side. I have no reservations about shooting him if necessary, but I hope it doesn't come to that. I don't have an appetite for killing a fellow countryman and agent, especially when I do not yet know where his loyalties lie.

"Where are we going?" Mélon asks.

"Shut up and walk."

"Whatever you—" He grunts as I push the tip of my pistol into his side.

Mélon is being very good, very pliant. What is he planning? I need to get him into a place where I have better control of the situation. Out here on the street, it is too easy for him to turn things on me. Fortunately, Bogdanova Fare is the next cross street, and at the corner I maneuver Mélon to the right and down a row of upscale townhouses to number eleven.

The outer door is unlocked and opens into a small entry and a narrow flight of dark stairs. I sweep the door shut behind us with my foot. It's cold and still enough in the foyer that our breath circles our heads like wraiths.

"The light," I say.

Mélon pulls the chain and a faint pendant bulb clicks to life.

I nod at the stairs, and Mélon starts up. I poke the pistol into the small of his back so he knows not to try anything, and I follow him to the upstairs landing where we find a single door. I put the door key on top of the wainscoting.

"Open it."

"This isn't needed, Calypto."

"Open it."

Mélon sighs in seeming resignation. He takes the key and thrusts it into the deadbolt. The lock clunks as the tumblers turn. He pushes the door open.

I reach around the jamb and locate the light switch.

"Whose place is this?" he asks.

I motion him into the apartment with a wave of my pistol then close the door behind us. Mélon stands awkwardly in the middle of a lavishly furnished living room. Heavy blackout curtains obscure the windows that look out onto Bogdanova Fare. The light filtering through the overhead fixture is a faint yellow, giving a warm glow to the apartment's rich carpets, soft lounges and wing chairs that sit before a fireplace with an impressive marble mantel.

"Nice place," Mélon says. The calmness of his tone tells me he's a man who has been at a gun's point before.

"We need to talk," I say.

"And then what happens?"

"I don't know. That depends on what you say."

"Fair enough. Shall we sit, then?"

"First, take out your weapon—very slow—and put it on the table."

Mélon does as he's instructed. "This isn't necessary," he says.

His words confirm to me that it is. I motion him away from the table and slip his weapon into the pocket of my long coat.

Mélon sits in one of the wing chairs and crosses his legs. He looks more gaunt than I remember from Coruşu, although many of my memories of that city are now muddled and vague. If I didn't know better, his pallor and sunken eyes would lead to me to believe him unwell. I remind myself not to let that make me complacent.

I sit on the edge of the couch and rest my weapon across my knees. I don't want to point it at Mélon, but I want him to be aware that it is still there, still a threat.

"You know, there really is no need for your weapon. We're all on the same side here, no?"

I allow the edges of my mouth to rise slightly.

"After Coruşu, I don't know who's on what side anymore."

Mélon frowns. "I heard about what happened to you."

"What have you heard?"

Mélon shrugs. "This and that, but I've learned not to trust what I hear unless I know the source."

"Entertain me."

Mélon's brow pinches together. It's almost imperceptible. He smooths it over so quickly most people would have missed it. He doesn't know what to tell me.

"General consensus is you have gone rogue," he says. "I think you've stolen something important, whatever you acquired from the auction in Coruşu. For whom, I don't know, but I hope they are paying you well."

I do not let my face betray any emotion, even though he has just accused me of treason. I would deny what he says, but that would only convince Mélon that he had the truth, which, except for the treason part, he does. I am still loyal to the Empire, and I will work toward its greater good. My problem is I don't know who else is doing the same. The Order? The Red Cuffs? The Silver Tigers, or whatever they are these days? In my business, few things are black and white, but at the moment, I'm awash in gray seas.

"You can't always trust what you hear," I say.

Mélon shrugs casually. "I take it you didn't bring me here at gun point to discuss your reputation."

"No. I want the envelope in your pocket."

"What envelope?"

"Don't play stupid with me. I can just as easily

shoot you and take it."

He doesn't consider my threat for long. "Let's not be hasty."

"Slowly," I say as he reaches into his coat and removes a manila envelope.

He holds it up. "My mission orders."

"Orders?"

Mélon looks at me askance.

The manila envelope certainly looks like all the ones I have received from R. If this is what Mélon says, inside will be an onion skin sheet with a typed set of orders and maybe a few other items that might be necessary to carry them out. But Mélon's envelope came from a Red Cuff.

"Show me."

Mélon unloops the red string holding the flap shut and slides out an onion skin sheet. Before he can read the page or otherwise do anything to it, I snatch it from his hand. He makes a sudden move toward me, but stops when my pistol comes up to his neck. He holds up his hands, the envelope still in his left, and settles back into the chair.

Within several glances I confirm that the paper is indeed a set of orders, just like those I might have received from R.

"You see," Mélon says. "Orders. Nothing more. Nothing less."

But they can't be real orders, unless Mélon is actually working for the Red Cuffs. "Who gave you these?"

"Who else?" he asks. "My handler."

Handler? He must not think I saw the exchange or he doesn't know that I recognized who gave him the envelope. But if he's in on what happened in Corușu, then he must know that I've seen Katalin Kovac. He must know that I would recognize her.

"Since when did you start working for the Red Cuffs?"

Mélon spits a curse. It sounds genuine, but that doesn't mean it is. "I don't work for them."

"I saw the woman who gave these to you. She works for the Red Cuffs."

Mélon laughs—a deep, genuine laugh. "You're a fool, Calypto. You don't know what you're talking about." Mélon stops laughing and his brow pinches together.

"Yes," I say. "I must be mistaken." I barely hear myself say the words. They come out almost automatically. Perhaps neither of us knows what we are talking about, but I cannot dismiss the possibility that we are both correct and Katalin Kovac is a both Red Cuff and not a Red Cuff. I am reminded of a story told by one of my instructors when I first joined The Order. Two men stand in the night looking at a statue. One says, 'Impressive carving of a crouching lion.' The second frowns and says, 'It's not a lion, but two men wrestling.' So, which man is right? They are both right, based on the information they have. The angle from which they view the statue, the light, their experiences—has the second man ever seen a lion?-all affect their perception of the truth. As far as both men are concerned, what they see is true. And it is true within the confines of their reality. But which man is correct? What *is* the statue? That quickly becomes a philosophical question. One, both, or neither man could be correct, but in truth that doesn't matter, because each man is convinced his answer is right.

"Do you mind if I smoke?" Mélon asks.

"Don't," I say curtly.

Mélon tucks his cigarettes back into his coat pocket and settles back into his chair still holding the manila envelope on his lap.

What does this mean about Katalin Kovac? I knew it was an alias, but I always assumed she was a Red Cuff. I still think she is, but then how do I explain the orders I'm holding? Mélon could be Red Cuff, but I do not accept that because my orders for Coruşu, which came directly from R's hands, had me meet up with him. That brings me back to Katalin Kovac. In Coruşu, Krauss had acquiesced to her as if she was his superior, and I doubt he would have done that if he had known she was with The Order. The same would be true for Mélon accepting orders from her if he knew she was a Red Cuff. That leaves three options that could explain these seemingly conflicting realities: She's a Red Cuff who's infiltrated The Order, a handler who has infiltrated the Red Cuffs, or something else that has infiltrated both.

I freely acknowledge I am biased, but only one of those options is a plausible reality for me. Katalin Kovac is a member of The Order and for some unknown amount of time, she has been infiltrated into the Red Cuffs. She is Mélon's handler and thus must have given him his orders to meet me in Coruşu. Therefore, she must have known who I was at that auction, which can only mean that she is the mechanism through which my betrayal occurred.

The paper trembles in my hand.

What in hell is going on?

"You don't look so good," Mélon says smugly.

"Shut up." My mind races but gets nowhere.

I rise from the couch and move to the fireplace. I'm farther away from Mélon and can watch him more easily while I read the onionskin.

The orders look no different than the dozens I've seen previously, further supporting their authenticity. They are typed, the letters dark and heavy as if they had been applied to the onionskin with a hammer and punch instead of extruded from a teletype. Succinct, as always, and in this case five lines:

> BEGIN TRANS
> Immediate Action Req
> Secure: Gorelov, Anton
> Return, Report
> END TRANS

My brow pinches together. A retrieval order for a Mr. Anton Gorelev. Gorelov? That name sounds familiar to me, but I come across a lot of names in my work. I wonder what he's done to draw the scrutiny of The Order.

"What else is in the envelope?"

My question startles Mélon, and he drops the envelope onto the floor. As he bends over to retrieve it, I'm shaken by a jolt of vertigo and stumble back against the fireplace mantel. The world stutters to a momentary halt; the dust hanging in the light takes on the sharpness of pin tips, the floral pattern of the carpet the crispness of crystalized sugar, and Mélon's hand inches toward a barely perceptible lump under the edge of his trouser leg.

A vase tumbles in slow motion off the mantel. It accelerates, shattering on the brick hearth as the world leaps forward. Already I am in motion. Metal glints as Mélon sweeps his hand toward me. A small knife whistles past my ear and thunks into a painting above the mantel shelf.

I tumble across the floor and roll back to my feet, raising my FP, but Mélon is already out of his chair. He sweeps his left foot upward, striking my weapon with the heel of his boot. Fortunately, he doesn't hit my hand—the force of the blow could have broken it—and I manage to keep hold of my pistol. Before I can use it, however, Mélon is on me, and all I can do is fend off his flurry of blows aimed at my throat—a set of rapid combinations, like I've never seen before. I fend most off completely, but several I can only deflect. One numbs my shoulder with its force, and another grazes my left cheek, opening a small cut beneath the corner of my eye. Sometime during the exchange, my pistol is lost.

But I'm still standing, having survived his initial, brutal assault.

I retreat a half-dozen steps in an attempt to regain my composure. Mélon presses forward, giving me no chance to regroup. He's a better hand-to-hand fighter than I am, and it's only a matter of time before one of his shots gets past my defenses. If one of his punches hits me square in the throat, it will kill me.

I fend off another rapid combination, and this time instead of retreating, I lunge forward to get inside his reach. Before he can sidestep me, I slam into him and the two of us tumble to the ground, locked together. We roll across the floor, coming to a stop near the fireplace. Pieces of the shattered vase grind under my back. Mélon is on top of me, trying to free his hands, but I keep them tied up while shifting my weight around, trying to unbalance him. He gets his left hand free and slaps me in the face. The blow doesn't hurt so much as sting, but it makes my eyes water.

I look away and his punch grazes past my ear. His fist thumps loudly into the floor, and he grunts in pain. I hope he's shattered a knuckle, but it's a wishful thinking as he cocks his fist back again.

I jab at his face, but in my position, I can't deliver a blow with much force behind it. It's enough to distract him, however, giving me a chance to deliver a second. I hit him in the nose this time, and the cartilage cracks with a pop. A third blow hits bone—his cheek maybe—and, sensing Mélon is off balance, I shift my weight violently to the side, forcing him off me and toward the fireplace. His head strikes the stonework, and he crumples to the floor, lying partially inside the firebox.

Mélon doesn't move.

I sit up on my knees, breathing heavily. The knuckles on my right hand hurt and are already swelling up. Blood traces a line down my cheek, and I wipe at it to stop it from staining my collar. The cut is minor, but later the bruising might not be.

I retrieve my weapon and snatch a lace doily off a table that I press against the cut on my face. I nudge Mélon's foot with my own. It moves without resistance. He hit the stonework hard; at minimum, he's knocked out. At worst, he's...I don't want to go there. I never meant to hurt him, but he gave me no choice. He, at least, was attacking to kill.

I grab one of his ankles and drag him out of the fireplace. Other than his nose, Mélon isn't bleeding from anywhere else, but he has a large knot growing on the back of his head where he hit the stones. His breathing is faint, but steady.

I curse. This is a complication of my own making. What did I expect to happen? Mélon and I would talk and we'd be friends at the end? That's the problem— I wasn't thinking; I was reacting. Perhaps Mélon unconscious in the fireplace is not such a bad outcome. Unfortunately, it is a temporary solution. At some point, Mélon is going to wake.

The apartment has only a handful of rooms and isn't the type of place where I would expect to find a coil of stout rope. It has the look of a wealthy business magnate's second home—perhaps a place for a Ordinburg businessman to stay when in Aurestapol. The kitchen is poorly stocked and the small pantry is empty except for dozen bottles of assorted wine and a bottle of high-end vodka.

I slip the vodka bottle into my long coat pocket. I have a feeling I will want it later.

The only other room is the bedroom, but a search of the bedside table turns up an assortment of padded leather restraints, gags, and silk-lined blindfolds. I arch an eyebrow at the lascivious find, but to each their own, I guess. I snap the restraints between my hands and decide they will do.

For a wiry man, Mélon is heavy, but I manage to get him onto the bed. I secure his wrist to the headboard—it has two stout rings attached to it just for this purpose, I assume—and use another set of restraints for Mélon's ankles. Turning out his coat and trouser pockets, I find them empty other than a few bills in a money clip and an extra cartridge for his FP, both of which I take. I leave him covered with a blanket and will figure out what to do with him later.

I collapse onto the couch. My hands shake as I

toss back a shot of the vodka. It goes down smooth and warm, and my tension begins to bleed away. I start to pour another, but stop myself. I haven't eaten in a while, and I can't afford to get drunk, although that holds a certain attraction at the moment. I pour a half shot and slide the bottle away from me on the coffee table. The second drink takes the edge off my adrenaline rush. The trembling in my hands subsides.

The immediate danger is gone, but the encounter with Mélon only reinforces my greater danger. I'm used to danger, sure; it comes with the profession, but I'm not used it coming from one of my own.

Let's say for argument's sake I accept Katalin Kovac is Mélon's handler, and thus my presence wasn't simply leaked to the Red Cuffs, but that my imprisonment and torture was actively orchestrated by a fellow agent. I had already figured out this was about more than simply making me "gone," but my thinking about the *why* of it has always been restricted to the perspective of the Red Cuffs, thus I could never make sense of it. Now, the Red Cuffs appear to be only complicit fools in this plot. If The Order simply wanted me gone, a knife in the ribs and shallow grave in the woods would have been easier and cleaner. No one would have been any wiser, and few would have noticed me missing. Yet The Order didn't want me simply gone; they also wanted me branded a traitor. They wanted my reputation destroyed as much as me. Why?

One discredits another to destroy what others think of that person. If others are convinced I am a traitor, it would cast doubt on everything I had ever said and done.

I sit up suddenly.

Someone in The Order is worried about something I know. Something big. Something true. Likely something about The Order? But I don't know anything, except some cryptic references made by Alexei before he was gunned down in the Green Door Café in Olesk by—

My breath leaves me. Krauss killed Alexei. Was that also on orders from Katalin? And what about Dai Li? I assume she is also dead by Krauss's hand.

I retrieve the onionskin and the manila envelope from the floor. Inside the envelope is a single page dossier on Anton Gorelov, and nothing else. After feeling around, I discover nothing stuck to the sides of the envelope. This seems like an awfully thin package for a secure-and-return mission.

The bust shot attached to the single sheet looks like an official portrait someone might get for traveling papers. Gorelov's small eyes squint directly into the camera with no hint of a smile on his face. He looks to be middle-aged, although it is hard to tell given he is completely bald. He looks underwhelming in every way, although I've learned to never underestimate someone's mettle based on his appearance. I unclip the photo from the dossier and set it aside.

Hmmm... I was right. Age forty-eight, or so the half page of information tells me. He's taller than I imagined from the picture, married with two children, and he has a flat on the east side of Korelov Lake in a neighborhood popular with government officials. Government? I get the feeling again that I should know this name. I quickly skim through the rest of the information, and sure enough, he works for the Ministry of Ethics and Culture.

Gorelov... Gorelov. I'm certain now that I've heard the name before. Then it hits me like a blow from a lead pipe. When I had last seen Odella, she had told me about an Anton Gorelov with whom she had worked during her time at the Inspector General's Office. He had been involved in the investigation they were conducting on The Order back when Odella and I had first met. Gorelov was one of the few men beside the Emperor who would have seen the Inspector General's review before the investigation had been buried unexpectedly without being completed.

This had to be more than coincidence. The Order wants Gorelov off the street—or at least Katalin Kovac and whomever she is working with does.

I reread The Orders. It is a secure-and-return mission, not an elimination. The Order doesn't want him dead, at least not yet, but they want him off the street quickly. Why so quickly? Likely because someone else wants him too, and The Order wants to—or maybe *has* to—get there first.

I likely don't have much time if I am going to get to him before anyone else.

PART II

ASHES OF DESPERATION

IF I WERE SMART, I would have stuck Mélon in the claw foot tub and made it look like he slit his own wrists, but I have no stomach for killing one of our own. R would have chastised that sentimentality—it's what gets good agents killed—but murdering Mélon without proof he has betrayed the Empire would mean I've accepted the corruption within The Order is systemic and not restricted to a few agents. Mélon may be one of the bad guys, but he also might not, and in The Order I believe in, that distinction is important. Perhaps, even after all these years, I am naïve.

Instead, I leave him tied to the bed, gagged and blindfolded. I'll arrange his release once my business in Aurestapol is finished and I'm safely away. I don't plan to be here long.

Stepping out onto Bogdanov Fare, I pull the collar of my long coat up around my ears and push my hat tighter on my head. Thick clouds obscure the moon, but its faint blue glow illuminates the empty sidewalk. Otherwise the city is dark. Aurestapol may be far from the fronts, but fears of an enemy air raid still run high among the populace, no matter how unlikely that may be. The Emperor's ministers have done the calculations and concluded the dark nights and deep rationing may suck away the city's morale, but better this than the panic that would result if the city were to be bombed by Papalate airships, no matter how slim that chance.

Fortuitous for me, however; empty streets and curtained windows mean no prying eyes, but the police will still be watching for those who break curfew. I stick to the alleyways running parallel to the main avenues. After twenty minutes, I come into a bourgeois district of brick townhouses and wide, tree-lined sidewalks. From beneath one of the chestnuts on the opposite side of the street, I survey Gorelov's house. The brick-faced, two-story home has stout, leaded-glass windows framed with intricate stonework. A delicate wrought iron fence surrounds a small patch of grass in the front. According to the dossier, Gorelov has been home for nearly an hour already, but with its heavy blackout curtains, the house looks dark and unoccupied.

I have been so focused on getting here; now that I stand outside I don't know exactly what my plan is. Am I trying to keep him away from The Order and whoever else might be about to show up or simply learn what he knows? I assume The Order already knows what Gorelov knows—his investigation concluded a decade ago—and they want him secured so he can't tell anyone else. Who might that anyone else be? The Silver Tigers come to mind immediately. While that group may be divided on the method to achieve their goal, they are committed to destroying

The Order. I suspect the Tigers associated with Dai Li and Alexei knew about Gorelov. Perhaps they have even spoken with him already. By all experience, the other faction of the Silver Tigers, the one led by Valentin, is the more problematic of the two. According to Dai Li, Valentin's solution for The Order is an unhealthy end to everyone associated with it. While Gorelov is not part of The Order, he must know a great deal about it. That information in the wrong hands could prove deadly.

Mélon likely intended to intercept Gorelov before he arrived at home. That would have been easy on a dark street. Now that Gorelov is home, I'll have to contend with his family, too. Alternatively, I could wait until morning and intercept him as he heads to work, but the urgency in Mélon's orders suggests I may not have the luxury of time.

I have to do this now.

If I can get him to open the door, I can try a straight-forward approach. He's investigated The Order, so he must know who we are. If he's accepted that much then he might accept my story of intrigue and danger. I might even persuade him to help me voluntarily. If that fails, I can always flash my FP and threaten to rob his loving family of their husband and father unless he comes quietly with me. Either way, the key for me is to get this behind closed doors, which will be easier if I'm *invited* inside.

After a few deep breaths to settle dissenting thought, I cross the street and open the gate. With the street lamps out, Gorelov's stoop is shadowy, and I doubt anyone not specifically looking in that direction would even see me. The stout door has a knocker that looks like it might be a ring held in the mouth of a bear, but it's hard to say with certainty in the dimness. I forego the knocker and rap lightly on the stout wood with my knuckle. If anyone is downstairs, I expect they should hear it, but I doubt the sound would carry upstairs. I count five and rap a little harder. Still no answer.

Perhaps he has already retired to the upstairs and cannot hear me. I relent and use the knocker.

I press my ear to the door, but hear no movement inside. Given the shortages of coal and the blackout orders, many citizens take to their beds early rather than sit in the cold trying to live life by meager candlelight.

Time for a new plan.

I circle around to the rear service alley. All the townhouses have a rear door for deliveries. Perhaps I can quietly force my way in, or maybe gain access through a carelessly secured coal chute. As I go up the alley, I count the doors until I come to Gorelov's.

I remove my FP and pressurize the chamber. I hope I won't need the weapon, but better prepared than caught off guard. I take care to avoid the rubbish bins as I approach the door and press my ear against it. As my head touches the wood, the door slides open. I jump away, raising my pistol.

In the darkness, I run my right hand along the door frame. It's splintered where the bolt used to be. The outer frame is dented where a pry bar has been used.

I loose a muffled curse. Someone has beaten me here and already gained entry.

I nudge the door with my foot.

The faint moonlight coming in reveals a modest-sized kitchen that appears well kept except for a few dishes on the counter near the sink. A large samovar glints in the faint blue light from atop a small table pushed against one wall. The room is warm and smells faintly of baked bread.

I carefully close the door behind me to keep the cold out. As the room darkens, I pause to let me eyes adjust further, but in the near blackness, they can't adjust much. Everything is grainy and shadowy. I search forward with my hearing.

A clock ticks in room toward the front of the house.

A floor plank squeaks lightly as I move toward the door to the hallway. At the doorway, I peer around the corner, but see nothing—the interior of the house is much too dark.

I edge forward, feeling my way into the darkness with the toe of my boot. If I can get to the front of the house, I can open one of the blackout curtains and allow some moonlight in. I slide along, back to the wall of the hallway, a slow half-step at a time. I come to a narrow table and maneuver around it, taking care not to knock over anything adorning it. On the other side of the table is another doorway.

I pause here to collect my breath. I'm sweating heavily, and I can barely hear the clock over the sound of my pulse pounding in my ears. Otherwise the silence presses against me like water. Perhaps whoever broke in has left. Maybe I'm too late, and Gorelov and his family have already been taken or worse.

I chide myself. Don't jump to conclusions, and focus on the task at hand.

The ticking clock is through the doorway in what I assume to be a front sitting room. I peer in, but as with the rest of the house, it is too dark to make out anything but grainy, shadowy shapes. I hold for a three count, and when nothing moves, I step cautiously into the parlor.

I pull aside the edge of the blackout curtain just enough to let sufficient moonlight into the room for me to see the couch and a pair of wingback chairs, several tables, and an ornate fireplace. While slightly more mundane, Gorelov's parlor looks similar to the one on Bogdanov Fare, giving me an unsettling sense of déjà vu.

A shaft of moonlight spotlights the contents on one of the small tables. In the center, prominent and large, sits a family portrait. The man is Gorelov; his bald head is unmistakable. His wife is much shorter than him, with a solid, round face and light hair pulled up into a bun. She looks like a farmer's wife, not the spouse of a ranking government bureaucrat. It isn't these two who catch my eye, however. It's the children. The two boys couldn't be more than three or four. Their dark hair and slender features look nothing like Gorelov or his wife's. Given the children's young age and appearance, I doubt they are the Gorelov's biological progeny. Not that this is unusual during these times. Many children have been orphaned by the ravages of war. Most have been tossed into the state system, which is a rough turn of life. That Gorelov and his wife would rescue two from that fate casts him in a brighter light for me.

Floor boards creak, yanking me back into Gorelov's parlor. I spin, raising my FP, but no one is behind me.

Another creak, coming from directly overhead.

I edge toward the parlor door. The corridor

leading from the kitchen in the back of the house opens into a front foyer with a flight of stairs. I slide along the wall toward the front door, straining to see up the stairs. I press myself into the corner of the foyer, hidden in the shadows. I wipe my palm on my long coat.

Another creak.

It can't be Gorelov. Whoever is moving around upstairs is likely the person who pried open the rear door. But are Gorelov and his family upstairs with this intruder? Are they even still alive? The thought of murdered children raises angry bile into my throat.

If this intruder has harmed the children, he will pay dearly.

I'm about to move toward the stairs when the door lock clicks and rotates. The handle turns and the door starts to open.

My breath leaves me, and I push myself back into the shadows. My mind frantically explores options, but I realize I have none.

Footsteps move across the ceiling toward the top of the stairs.

The door swings open. A tall person in a coat and hat crosses the jamb, his hand sliding up the wall to the pull cord for the ceiling lamp.

I grab his wrist and yank firmly. With a startled yelp, the man tumbles to the floor in the direction of the parlor door, his hat flying off to reveal a bald head.

Gorelov.

His identity barely has time to register as fletchettes splinter the wooden frame and ricochet off the edge of the door. One catches my right arm, just above my elbow, slicing through my coat and tearing my skin. I stumble and fall back against the wall. My arm burns from the grazing wound.

Several more fletchettes thunk into the wood where my neck had been a moment before.

I squeeze off several poorly aimed shots as I tumble to the floor. Another fletchette cuts the top of my shoulder but doesn't hit me square enough to cause much more than a wasp sting. I scramble across the floor toward the parlor door, grabbing and dragging Gorelov by the nape of his coat as I go.

Heavy footfalls rattle the stairs as my attacker bounds down in giant strides.

Gorelov is frozen, and I'm unable to drag him more than a meter or two.

"Move or die," I say, turning and shooting into the darkness near the stairs. Fletchettes whistle from my FP, splintering off the wooden bannister.

My words must have registered because Gorelov scuttles into the parlor.

Fletchettes hum by my ear and shatter the glass pane of the parlor door. Based on the pitch, these are large-caliber projectiles capable of disabling or killing with a single direct hit. My assailant is using a military-grade weapon.

I retreat into the parlor as my attacker hits the landing at the bottom of the stairs.

I shoot behind me without aiming, hoping to buy myself a desperate moment.

The faint moonlight gleams off Gorelov's head as he scrambles into the adjacent dining room.

I dash across the parlor and grab Gorelov from behind by the belt of his coat and pull him against the wall, just inside the dining room door. He's panicked, and I struggle to keep him there. If I didn't need him conscious, I'd strike him with the butt of my pistol, but there is no way I can carry him and deal with our attacker.

I slap him hard across the jaw, hoping to rattle some sense back into him. It seems to work. At least he's not struggling anymore. Instead he's staring glassy-eyed into the darkness— frozen, as if the world has simply stopped moving forward through time.

I am tossed with a sense of vertigo, and I realize almost too late what is happening. The world, stuck for a brief moment, begins to accelerate forward again, but in that second, I let my weight drop to the ground, pulling Gorelov down with me by his lapel. As I'm falling, I see the three slivers of metal accelerating through the air, catching a glint of moonshine as they blur back to full speed and blast into the plaster wall where Gorelov and I were a half second before.

We slam onto the floor planks. The blow numbs my left knee, and Gorelov tumbles into the chairs around the table in the center of the room.

Our assailant has circled around, and come into the dining room from the corridor. I try to get a bead on him, but he's around the table before I can level my weapon. He's a huge man, the size of bear. His nose glistens in the bluish light, like a flattened fungus sprouting from the bark of a forest tree. His mouth is framed by a scrabbly black beard that drinks the light.

I know this face.

He is the Silver Tiger assassin who killed Alexander Olstevski. I witnessed it on the same cold morning I headed to Olesk, the very mission when all of my current problems seemed to take root.

The muzzle of his weapon comes around. It's an

extended-barrel FP, the likes of which I have never seen before, and he has me dead in his sights. The weapon discharges, but at the same time, Gorelov must have kicked out and struck the bear man in the back of the knee because the barrel of his weapon comes up suddenly and the fletchettes thunk into the floor planks a hand's breadth above my head.

With the bear man off balance, I am able to sweep his feet from under him, and he tumbles back against the table, but doesn't fall to the floor. I strike out a second time with my boot, scoring a solid hit to his groin that doubles him over and draws forth a throaty outburst.

My own weapon comes around, and I squeeze the trigger, puffing a blast of air, but nothing more because the cartridge is empty.

I scramble forward, swinging the weapon with as much force as I can, and I deliver a brutal blow to the side of the bear man's head. He staggers away from the table and trips over Gorelov still on the floor. He tumbles over, landing with his weapon pinned under his great bulk. The blow was hard enough to have killed many men, but it seems to have only stunned him.

Unbelievably, he is already moving to get back to his feet.

I grab Gorelov by the collar and pull him upright as I head back into the parlor toward the front door. Gorelov follows without argument.

As I pull the front door open, a pair of autos whirrs to a stop in front of Gorelov's townhouse, and several Red Cuffs climb out.

I push Gorelov back inside, hissing for him to go the rear door. When he doesn't follow me, I drag him by the coat again to get him moving. In the dark corridor, I crash into the narrow table standing along the wall, and Gorelov squeezes by me and slips into the kitchen as the bear man enters the hallway from the dining room. His weapon hisses as I drop behind the narrow table and the heavy fletchettes ricochet off the plaster and wainscoting, showering splinters and dust onto my head.

I grab the narrow table by the legs and upend the remaining knickknacks. I hold it in front me like a shield and charge down the hallway.

Fletchettes chunk loudly into the table's surface, but I don't slow. In the narrow corridor, the bear man has nowhere to go, and I crash into him. The blow knocks me backward, and I fall to the floor, the table splinters and clatters to my left. The bear man is also knocked back, and he tumbles into the dining room. I scrabble across the floor into the kitchen as the front door bursts open and Red Cuffs storm into the house.

Gorelov is already out the rear door, and I burst out into the darkened alleyway and skitter to a stop on the uneven cobblestones. Gorelov is halfway down the alley, running as fast as he can.

I hesitate, looking toward the windows of the upper floors of the townhouse. How can Gorelov flee when his wife and children are still up there? Sure, they are likely dead—I heard no sounds of movement other than the bear man—but how would Gorelov know that?

Voices inside the house shake my mind back to the danger at hand.

Whether they are alive or dead, there is nothing I can do for his family, so I sprint after Gorelov, reloading my FP as I go. I need to catch him before he gets to the main street where he could be seen by the Red Cuffs or anyone else who might intend him harm.

Seemingly out of immediate danger, Gorelov's adrenaline rush fades and his sprint slows to a walk. Clouds of breath burst from him, and as I reach him, he stands with his hands on his hips watching me approach.

"Who...are—"

I grab him by the arm and force him to the side of the alley, behind a collection of rubbish bins.

"Did you get hit?" I ask in a hoarse whisper.

He struggles to catch his breath. "No. I...don't think so."

If he had been, he would know.

"Who are—"

I put my right index finger to my lips—the action makes my arm burn. In the struggle, I did not have the luxury to feel my wounds, but now, as my adrenaline ebbs, they make their presence known. Neither wound feels particularly serious, but that doesn't mean they are not painful.

"There is nothing we can do for your family," I say. "We need to get out here."

"My family? They're not here, but—"

"They are away?" This is good news, for now.

"Yes, they are—"

I shove Gorelov deeper into the shadows as the bear man appears suddenly in the alleyway. He turns away from us and starts running, disappearing quickly into the night. A second later, two Red Cuffs burst into the alleyway in pursuit, but I know they are no match for the bear man's speed. The Red Cuffs have no chance of catching him, but they will catch Gorelov and me if we stay here.

"Now is not the time. We must move." The bear man has gone the way we would need to go to return to R's safehouse. Given the additional Red Cuff pursuit, that direction is no longer a viable option. That means circling around, and it's now well past curfew. While not impossible for those with luck or experience, I'm not willing to bet Gorelov has much of either right now. We'll need to find a closer option.

"What is—" Gorelov starts, but I shush him once more. Deterred for only a moment, however, he starts again. Fortunately, he has the wherewithal to whisper. "I'm not going anywhere until you tell me what's going on."

He doesn't realize the depth of the danger he's in. "If you walk, my word I'll explain."

A cold wind cuts through my long coat, and Gorelov hunkers down into his collar. Having lost his hat in the struggle, he must be cold. I would give him mine, but the threat of frostbite might get him moving.

In the moonlight, his eye twitches.

"You can return to your home, which is currently occupied by Red Cuffs."

"I've done nothing wrong. I'm the victim here."

"And I'm sure you'll be able to convince the Red Cuffs of that," I say, pausing just long enough to achieve the desired effect before adding, "given enough time."

Gorelov nods, and I motion him down the alley.

"Give me your handkerchief," I say. Any man of Gorelov's stature surely carries one. He starts to say something, but I cut him off. "Just give it to me."

Gorelov digs into his pocket and hands me a dark cloth.

I press it against my right arm as we walk.

We stay in the shadows along the edge of the ally and move quickly. At the mouth of the alley, I peer into the cross street. To our right, a Red Cuff auto blocks the intersection to Gorelov's street. I can't see the Red Cuffs, but I assume they are nearby. Crossing the street to continue down the service alley would be risky, so I turn us away from the Red Cuffs and hustle along the sidewalk. Gorelov hurries to keep up with me.

"Where are you taking me?" Gorelov asks.

"Away from here," I say. I don't have a destination in mind, but the sooner we get off the street, the better. That is reinforced when a *mussor* foot patrol crosses our path a block ahead of us, forcing us to freeze so as not to attract their attention. One of the *mussor* pauses and looks in our direction, but we're far enough away the darkness hides our motionless forms.

I exhale heavily once they continue.

"You're going to get us arrested," Gorelov says.

I ignore his protest. "Come on." I pull his coat sleeve, and he grudgingly follows.

We cross a major boulevard and turn into the next available alleyway. A few blocks east, Gorelov's neighborhood of brick stone townhouses gives way to several blocks of crumbling tenements and narrow, uneven streets. The dilapidated buildings are still occupied—I hear the noises of life within as we pass—but one of them is empty, having been gutted by a fire. The doors are missing and the windows are broken. The metal handrail looks as if it has been pried from the entry stoop, likely scavenged for the war effort.

"In here," I say bounding up the steps. The heat has spalled the stonework, and cinders grind under my boots.

"In there?" Gorelov covers his nose. The smell of recently burnt timbers is acrid and strong.

"It's out of the wind," I say. We may be able to build a fire inside, one whose light can't be seen from the street, but I don't want to make a promise to Gorelov I might not be able to keep.

A stiff gust of wind convinces Gorelov to follow me into the building. Broken glass, charred timbers, and the remnants of furniture and other household belongings litter the inside. In many places, the ceiling has been burned through, revealing the upper floors, but at least the thick planks on the ground floor are still solid. The soot and burnt wood seem to absorb what little moonlight there is, leaving the interior as dark as it is still.

I head toward the back of the ruin, navigating carefully through the debris. The doors off the corridor are either missing or open, but it's too dark to see anything beyond the black openings.

The smell of the fire grows stronger, and I realize this isn't just the stink of old charred wood. It's fresh smoke—just a trickle and not enough that someone on the street would be able to separate it from the smell of the burned building. It's coming from the end of the hallway.

"Stay here," I whisper.

I creep down the hallway, stepping carefully so as not to crunch the debris. As I near the stairwell, I stay close to the wall. A fire pops loudly, echoing tinnily. I peer around the corner. In the space beneath the remnants of the stairs, two men huddle around a metal washtub, covered with a sheet of tin. The tin sheet fits tightly enough atop of the tub to block all but a faint glow from the fire, just enough to allow me a decent look at the two men warming themselves.

One is short and stocky; the other is about my height and more gangly than his comrade. They both wear old coats, and their threadbare caps are pulled over long, stringy hair. Their outstretched hands are wrapped in strips of cloth.

Rascals.

There are many desperate men these days, what with the war and the shortages. Desperate men are generally dangerous men too.

I start to back away and a cinder pops under my boot. I mouth a curse as I freeze. I don't dare breathe, hoping their fire is loud enough to cover the noise.

"It's cold, friend, and our fire is big enough to share." The words are hoarse, as if the speaker's throat has been ripped raw by decades of cigarette smoke.

I don't move, willing the silence to convince them they were mistaken. I tighten my grip on my FP, just in case they decide to come investigate.

"Now you're just being rude," the man says. I hear a scraping sound, like a metal bar being picked up.

I can't afford to get into a fight. After everything that has already happened, I'm not sure how Gorelov will respond.

"Okay, I'm coming out," I say. I shove my FP into

the pocket of my coat and raise my hands. As I step into view of the stairwell, one of the men pushes back the tin sheet, releasing the light from the metal tub.

The short man has a wild fringe of whiskers along his jawline. In his right hand is a metal pry bar, but it isn't raised. "That's better now, isn't it?" he asks, appraising me.

From where I stand, the warmth of the fire beckons. I fight the urge to enter. There are only two of them, but the space is small, and I'm sure these two are tougher than they look, but I am cold, and my Talent senses nothing. If danger lurks here, it is not imminent.

"You have room for two," I ask, "or should we just move on?"

Their eyes sparkle red as they eye me suspiciously.

In my long coat and with my scruffy beard, I could play the part of a rascal. If these two will accept that, I don't know, but they shuffle around the fire to make room for me.

I call for Gorelov to approach, and then I step up to the washtub, taking the spot that would put me between Gorelov and the hallway. I eye the two men, trying to decipher intent from their expressions. The tall one doesn't make eye contact, but the one who spoke locks me with a defiant glare. I slowly extend my hands, giving him what I hope he will take as a thankful nod.

My two comrades look worse up close than they did from the stairwell entrance. Their leathery faces are wind burnt, their hair unkempt, and their coats are filled with as many holes as crude patches of mismatched fabric. The tall one's front teeth are broken off, as if he's been hit in the mouth with a truncheon, which is probably not far from the truth.

Both of them look too old to have been drafted for the recent conflict, and from their appearance likely have been on the wrong side of luck for some time.

Gorelov comes around the corner and stops abruptly.

"Come warm yourself, Anton," I say.

Gorelov hesitates. Intentional or not, it is a good and appropriate response for the situation, but then he comes forward into the fire's pleasant bubble of warmth. I make room for him to step past me, and he doesn't seem to realize I have placed him such that I block his only exit from the stairwell.

The short man repositions the tin sheeting and the light drops once again to a faint, orange glow. "Not seen you before," he says. His left eyelid droops at half-mast, and the small scar at its corner glows smooth and red.

"Tough times," I say. It's a mantra for most, and these two accept it with knowing nods.

The short one scratches his beard, shedding flakes of skin that dance upward in the heat currents. His comrade shifts his weight from foot to foot, watching me from the corner of his eye.

"We're not deserters," I say. Men who have fled the front have little option but to exist at the frayed edges of society. They are hunted by the army, and if caught face execution. As such, they seldom go willingly, and I imagine the army and any *mussor* patrols have become accustomed to shooting first and asking questions later, a poor combination for innocent men simply down on their luck.

At my admission, the tall one visibly relaxes. The

short one makes an unconvinced grunt, but issues no challenge. Instead, he shifts his gaze to Gorelov and says, "What's your story, comrade?"

Gorelov's eye twitches. "Tough times," he says without looking up.

Well done. The less Gorelov says here, the better. From his coat and clean shave, it is plain Gorelov is no pauper.

The short one squints at him as he sucks at his teeth.

"Anton *used* to clerk for Talinder's Mercantile," I say, hoping it's enough to explain away the short one's doubts.

We fall into silence.

The night grows colder on my back.

The fire crackles under the tin. Its warmth bleeds through the front of my long coat and the toes of my shoes. The numbness retreats from my fingertips. My shoulder and right arm ache from their wounds, but I think the bleeding has stopped.

Several times Gorelov glances at me. While the situation is uncomfortable, we are likely safer here than on the streets.

"You do time in the west?" the short one asks.

I shake my head. "I'm not army material. I worked import until the business dried up." I leave it at that. A good cover story is short on details. If he wants more, I will provide it, but he seems to accept what I have offered.

"Anatoli was in the army." The short one nods toward his comrade. "Served the Empire in the Norden Conflict, didn't you, 'toli?"

The Norden Conflict was a bloody affair three decades ago with our northern neighbor, caused by a dispute over the ice-free harbor of Ordinburg. Following the collapse of Ordinburg as an independent city-state, the Empire annexed it, even though Norden had claimed historical right. Their claim was justified, best I can tell; most of Ordinburg's population was culturally descended from its northern neighbor, and given any say they would likely have joined that kingdom. As it did with the Romani highlands, the Empire saw the Ordinburg expansion as its divine destiny, but unlike Romani, it found itself entwined in a brief, but unfortunately bloody conflict.

Anatoli shrugs as if his service was an insignificant matter.

"'toli don't talk anymore," the short one says. "He took one in his neck; ripped his voice right out. Only by fate's grace did he not lose his breath, too."

I don't know what to say to that. His service to the Empire is admirable, but everyone serves at the grace of the Emperor and the land. My feelings, however, are not necessarily shared by all. Obviously, both these men have fallen on hard times, and Anatoli's situation may be a direct result of his service to his land. As a veteran, he should be cared for, but the veterans homes are no better than the state's orphanages. Every man who has served the Empire deserves a comfortable chair in front of a warm hearth and a hearty bowl of borscht to fill his insides.

"Has he no family?" Gorelov asks.

The short man grunts. "No family that cares. His wound left him damaged in the head, too, so he can't work and earn his way anymore."

"What about government services for veterans?"

The short man laughs.

I shake my head at Gorelov's naivety.

"This new war has overloaded the system," the short man says. "In with the new, out with the old." Contempt is clear in his voice. The current war has employed modern and terrible weapons, and an entire generation pays the price. The stagnant battlefields of the Westari front masticate our young like the diabolical gears of a terrible machine—ruined bodies, shattered minds, made doubly worse from the gases and chemicals. If the war keeps on for much longer, both sides will run out of young, able men and need to re-draft the old and return the infirmed and crippled to service just to keep the hostilities going. At this rate, the war will be won not through strategy and military superiority, but by simple attrition.

The short man has been railing about veterans' services, but he's incoherent, and half of what he says I can't hear over the popping of the fire in the washtub. He eventually winds down, and we stand quietly for a while.

"I'm sorry for what happened to your friend," I say to break the silence. "That should not happen. The Empire is built on backs like his, but the burden should not be so heavy that we break them. I am Ivan." I reach across the washtub. The column of heat is intense, even through the sleeve of my long coat. When the short man doesn't take my hand, I draw it back quickly. "Perhaps we should leave you to your fire."

I turn slowly away, but short man says, "Wait. It's cold out there, and times are tough for everyone. We'd be no better if we turned you away."

"Thank you," Gorelov says.

When I turn back, Anatoli is grinning at me, his

mental deficiencies now obvious.

"I am Sergei," the short man says.

My Talent is quiet, but my instincts tell me something is off. Over the past two years, the number of hard-luck people has increased rapidly throughout the Empire, especially in Aurestapol. Small tent cities rose up in the city's parks, but they didn't last long because *mussor* patrols initially started raiding the encampments. That drove the homeless into the sewers and the woods and the decaying sections of the city. I'm not sure if the *mussor* expected them to disappear. They have nowhere to go, no jobs, and, as Sergei notes, no help from the government whom many of them had served. Yet in a way, those enforcement actions served a purpose; they forced the undesirables out of sight, and gave the impression they no longer existed. Those with blinders could then choose to believe things weren't as bad as they were, but I don't think it fooled most. These *are* desperate times, and Anatoli and Sergei *are* desperate men. Men like them are not called rascals for being upstanding citizens.

I keep my left hand wrapped around the handle of my FP, and nearly draw it from my pocket when Anatoli reaches into his coat. But he only produces a bottle of vodka with what looks like a handkerchief stuffed into the opening. He drinks a swig and hands the bottle to Sergei.

Sergei holds the bottle up. "No top," he says as if in explanation, "so we best drink it before it spills." He tips the bottle against his lips. It's almost empty, but he doesn't finish it. He hisses and wipes his mouth with the back of his cloth-wrapped hand. "That's good, 'toli." He gives the vodka back to his comrade, and Anatoli extends it to Gorelov.

Gorelov studies the bottle skeptically, but takes it and puts it to his lips. He grimaces, likely not used to such low-quality alcohol. With a queasy expression, he hands the bottle to me.

If it had been fuller, I would have pretended to take a drink before passing it back Sergei, but only one swallow remains, so I drink it down. The vodka is harsh and burns my empty stomach like acid. I nearly cough it back up, but manage to keep it down.

Sergei laughs at my obvious displeasure. "Yes, 'toli, maybe these two are okay."

Anatoli grins his broken teeth.

"Did the *mussor* do that?" I ask.

Sergei grunts. "Rascals did. Bad as the *mussor*, them."

Sergei produces half a loaf of bread from his coat pocket. He breaks off about a quarter of it and offers it to me. I shouldn't eat their bread. They likely need it more than I do, but I suspect I would give insult by refusing their generosity, so I take it. Sergei tears off two more pieces and hands them around to Anatoli and Gorelov.

"I didn't steal this either," Sergei says, holding up his piece of crust. "Rascals steal, but I don't."

I nod my agreement, but say nothing. His conviction seems genuine, so who am I to question him.

"An old woman on Stanislav Avenue gives me the bread when I help her with her bags."

The bread is heavy and yeasty, sweetened slightly with honey. My stomach grumbles as I swallow, and I realize I haven't eaten since getting on the train yesterday afternoon. "What is your story, Sergei?" I ask, trying to make conversation.

Sergei shrugs as he chews. The flames have died down in the washtub, so the glow shining through crack between the tin and washtub lip is no longer as bright.

"The past is the past," says Sergei. "No sense dwelling on something that cannot be changed."

We all have regrets with which we must live. I decide not to push Sergei. "I have made choices I regret," I say. "I'd change them if I could, but..."

"Mmm, but the past is written."

"Yes."

We finish our bread in silence. The fire dies down further until the room is nearly dark and we are all barely shadows in the faint orange glow.

"Stay if you want," Sergei says after he and Anatoli have finished their bread. "But be warned, I sleep with one eye open." Sergei points to his drooping eyelid. Back in the corner, beneath the stairs, they have a shoulder pack and what appear to be a couple of bed rolls. They climb into them and the room is quiet except for the crackle and pop of coals and the occasional blast of wind through the doors and windows.

My preference is to leave. We have been fortunate so far, and I'm disinclined to test fate much longer, but I suspect leaving could be more dangerous than staying. The fire is well hidden from the street, and the bear man, the Red Cuffs, and *mussor* patrols are all out there. With the curfew, we lack the cover other people on the street would provide. I'm confident I could navigate these challenges alone, but with Gorelov as an additional package, I am much less certain. With no destination in mind, I am even more convinced that staying put until light is our best choice.

"We should make ourselves comfortable," I say quietly.

Gorelov stares at me as if I've said the words in a foreign tongue.

"It's too dangerous to be out at night," I say.

"I guess this is more comfortable than a Red Cuff interrogation room," Gorelov says, anticipating my next line. He speaks without humor, however, and his eye continues to twitch as he stares at me.

I settle onto the floor with my back to the wall, leaving the space in the corner for Gorelov. From that position, he will would need to step over me to get out of the stairwell. My resting spot also gives me clear view of Sergei's feet. I don't intend to sleep, but it would be foolish not to take every precaution possible, so I adjust my coat such that I can rest comfortably with my left hand in my pocket, fingers wrapped around the handle of my FP.

Gorelov joins me on the floor. Shivering, he pulls his coat's collar around his ears.

Soon the rough sounds of snoring emanate from the other side of the metal tub.

As if that is his cue, Gorelov says, "You promised to tell me what is going on. You can start by telling me who you are."

While events have taken an unexpected turn, I decide my original plan to tell him the truth hasn't changed. "My name is Ivan Titov, or at least that is one of my names. In The Order, I'm known as Calypto. I suspect you already know how The Order works."

"Counter Affairs?"

I haven't heard The Order called that since my first day of training. Counter Affairs is officially part of the Ministry of Security and Defense, but if you were to stop by the Counter Affairs office, you'd find it staffed by a dozen dedicated non-descript gray suits who put up a charade sufficient to satisfy any prying bureaucratic eyes. In actuality, or at least as I've been told, The Order doesn't answer to anyone up that particular chain.

"I see you've heard of it, perhaps from your time in the Inspector General's Office?"

"That was a long time ago. What is this about?"

"During your time with the Inspector General, you were involved in an investigation into The Or— Into Counter Affairs."

"I am not at liberty to discuss that or any past or current investigation."

"I understand," I say, trying to sound agreeable. I want him to tell me more, but he must trust me first if I'm going learn everything I can, not to mention keep him out of Katalin Kovac's hands. "I'm only asking because I'm concerned for your safety."

"How does an old government investigation affect my safety?"

"Knowledge of your involvement in that investigation has—how shall I describe it—fallen into undesirable hands, and these are not people who will respect the legal bounds of your silence."

"That man in my apartment. He wasn't some random criminal, was he?"

"He works for a group of revolutionaries whose goals conflict with those of the Empire."

"And the Red Cuffs?"

"When do Red Cuffs pay social calls? And before

you think they were there to help you, they had no knowledge of that assassin in your home." In truth, I am not sure how the Red Cuffs and bear man came to be there. Until this moment, I haven't had time to even think it through. Katalin issued the retrieval order to Mélon. Logic says it was in response to the Red Cuffs. Likely she would have heard about any Red Cuff directive to pick up Gorelov, and for whatever reason did not want him in Red Cuff hands. That would make bear man the less easily explained. How did he come to be there tonight?

"How do you fit into this?" If the light had been better, I'm certain I would have seen Gorelov's eyes proverbially narrow with suspicion.

Based on what I've told him to this point, it's a good question, and I suspect one that would have made R proud. I don't have a good answer, so I dig Mélon's onion skin from my coat pocket, and hand it to him.

"What's this?" he asks, because it's too dark for him to read it.

"I didn't know the assassin was in your home. I was there because The Order wants you off the street."

"So you're going to take me to them?"

I do not immediately answer, and sense Gorelov tensing.

I've started down this path of honesty, and see no reason to diverge from it now. "No. I'm...hmm...*persona non grata*, at the moment." I shake my head, but forge on as best I can. "I fear there is something wrong in The Order."

It's the first time I've said those words aloud. They sound as if they're coming out of someone else's mouth.

Gorelov makes a sound that tells me he's uncertain about everything.

"You don't want to run into bear man again," I say. "Between me and the Red Cuffs, I'm not your worst option." He doesn't respond as I gently take the onionskin from his hands and return it to my pocket. Based on his silence, I've not convinced him yet. I need to try a different approach. "Anton, where is your family?"

"Hmm?"

"Your wife and children, you said they are away."

"The Red Cuffs will go after them, won't they?"

Officially? No. In reality? That's the way they operate. Gorelov, their target, has slipped away from them, so I expect them to round up those he cares about to use as bargaining chips. His wife and children would be first in line for the honor. If that fails to move Gorelov, his family could simply disappear. Even I'm not sure what happens to those that disappear—I bet they end up in an unmarked grave, but maybe they're shipped off to stitch infantry boots at work camps in the northern wilds. Either way, I doubt Gorelov would ever hear from them again.

Gorelov doesn't wait for me to respond because he already knows the answer. "Can you get me to them? They are visiting my wife's parents outside of Ordinburg. If you get me to them, I will tell you what you want to know."

I take a deep breath and exhale it slowly. That's a tough request, especially given my current status and the resources at my disposal. I can't make that happen; not without help, and help is something lacking in my life right now.

"I won't let anything happen to my family," Gorelov says, his voice determined. "I will turn myself into the Minister's Internal Police if I have to."

"You can't trust the Red Cuffs."

"Right now, I think I trust them more than I trust you."

I find his words hard to argue with. Who am I to him? I've presented no concrete proof that I'm part of The Order, and even if I am, I've told him about my current status. For all he knows, I'll disappear the second he gives me what I want. The only thing keeping him here is the slim chance that I can do what he's asking.

"Tell me about that investigation, and I'll help you get to Ordinburg."

"No. Get me to Ordinburg, and then I'll tell you everything."

I don't see any way I can reasonably do that, especially on the timetable that would be needed. The Red Cuffs will be monitoring the trains and working their informants for any leads. It won't take them long to find us or to figure out where his family has gone. For all I know, they have already dispatched men to retrieve his wife and sons. The best we might be able to do is get a warning message to them, but I suspect that won't be sufficient to sway Gorelov to tell me all that he knows. It may be enough to save his family, however. Unfortunately, given the late hour and our current situation, sending a message is also simply not possible at this time.

It's then that I realize I want Gorelov to get back to his family. Call me soft, but any man willing to open his home to a couple of orphaned children can't be a bad person. My stomach sinks because I see no solution that guarantees a good outcome for any of them.

That leaves only my mission then, cold-hearted as that sounds.

"No deal," I say.

"Then turn me over to Counter Affairs."

The rapidity with which he responds suggests he anticipated my answer. He must already know I can't do that given my situation. Gorelov is a seasoned inspector and knows his way around an interrogation. He's calling my bluff, and no matter how I respond, he will learn much about his situation. And mine.

I should just lie to him, but I find that I can't. Even if I did lie to him, I suspect Gorelov's experience with professional liars would make that a risky gambit. I need to do something, but what?

"It's too dangerous to be on the streets during curfew," I say. "Get some sleep. We'll solve this tomorrow."

Gorelov makes a soft grunting sound. His coat rustles as a he turns away from me, and he burrows deeper into its collar for warmth.

For a while I sit there, trying to see a path through this impenetrable bramble. I might be able to drive him to Ordinburg, but I have no auto, and I suspect that will take longer than we reasonably have. What do I do if I still have no solution come morning and Gorelov tries to walk away from me? If I let him walk away, am I any worse off? He doesn't stand a chance out there. I suspect the Red Cuffs will get to him before bear man, but I doubt that option plays out any better for him, and likely worse.

Bear man...hmm. The same trifecta continues to

confront me. With everything that has happened this evening, I haven't had time to really think about the implications. Bear man is a Silver Tiger assassin, and based on what Dai Li has told me, he is aligned with Valentin's faction, who wants to see The Order and everyone in it exterminated. Yet, why kill Gorelov? He's not part of The Order, so his death does not make sense. In truth, taking Gorelov alive seems more useful to Valentin. Gorelov likely holds information about The Order that could make Valentin's job easier.

Maybe I have this all wrong.

I try to recall clearly what happened in Gorelov's town house, but the incident is a blur. Perhaps bear man was there to capture Gorelov, and only tried to kill him after I got involved, much like a Class A package in The Order. All Class A packages share two features: they contain information that is extremely important, and that information is also wanted by the enemy. Any agent entrusted with a Class A cannot let it fall into enemy hands, even if it means destroying the package. I thought I had been hidden, but my presence must have been detected by bear man. If true, then my being there triggered the shooting. This seems logical based on what I know. What I still don't know is how bear man came to be there tonight.

Coincidence? Maybe. For the most part, life is a procession of coincidences, drawing scrutiny only when they cause an unsettling disruption in our lives. Coincidence is an unsatisfying answer, however, and this combined with the assassination of Alexander Olstevski suggests Valentin's Silver Tigers may know an awful lot about things happening inside The

Order. An informant, perhaps?

The whole tangled web makes my head spin.

The pain in my shoulder and arm provides a welcome distraction. I probe the wounds through the tears in my long coat. The one on my shoulder just grazed the muscle, and is already covered with a sticky scab. A hand's width to the right, and I would have bled out from a perforated carotid. The wound on my right arm is deeper, but fortunately only cut the soft tissue, which on an arm tends to be mostly muscle. It's oozing again so I retie Gorelov's handkerchief, this time inside the sleeve of my long coat so it is not as obvious. Under better circumstances I'd get a half-dozen stitches, but I've done more with worse.

I stifle a yawn. Across the fire pot, Sergei's and Anatoli's snores rise above the crackle of the cinders. I don't trust them, and I should stay awake, but the warmth radiating from the fire and the draining adrenaline leave me tired. While I don't intend to sleep, my eyelids grow heavy. The floor isn't comfortable, but my aching body is tired. *You're a light sleeper*, my mind whispers dulcetly, and I find I cannot argue with it.

As a child in the orphanage bad things happened in the ward after lights outs, so being a light sleeper is strongly correlated with my survival. Not that the nocturnal ward was a merciless hunting ground to cull the weak and unpopular, but it was a time and place to settle any slights that rose above the level of revenge Mistress Markov would allow on her watch.

So I came awake quickly at the popping a cinder under the heel of a shoe. In a fluid motion born from years of training, I pull my FP from my long coat pocket and freeze Sergei in my sights as he leans over Gorelov.

I'm about to threaten him when my stomach suddenly churns, as if I were looking down from the open flight deck of a dirigible. A smile slides slowly across Sergei's face, as if the world is moving through molasses. A shadow eclipses the shine of his rheumy eye, and instinctively I roll. As the world surges forward, a metal pry bar accelerates forward and clangs against the stonework where my head was a second before.

I come to stop against a pair of old military boots. Nearly on my back, I look up the legs, between the arms holding the metal bar, and into Anatoli's grimacing face. His eyes widen in the gray dawn light. "Gah!"

Gorelov startles awake, throwing his hands up to protect himself.

Before Sergei can attack, I swing my legs around, and strike his ankle with enough force to sweep his feet from under him. Sergei crashes to the floor next to Gorelov with the solid sound of air leaving his lungs.

In that moment, Anatoli recovers from his surprise. His right boot rises to stomp on my head. I manage to fend it off with my left arm, and the boot's rough toe grazes my cheek and pounds the floor next to my ear. I try to raise my weapon, but Anatoli pins my left hand down with his foot. He re-cocks the pry bar. I wrap my right arm around his calf, and using Anatoli as leverage I swing my legs up and lock them around his thighs.

Unable to move his feet for balance, Anatoli is easily thrown to the ground where he tumbles across the floor and into the washtub. He cries out and curls into a ball as the hot metal burns his face.

I roll to my feet.

Gorelov has found his feet and presses into the corner, his fists raised, but not quite ready for a fistfight.

Sergei is on one knee, rubbing at his ankle.

I level my FP at his neck.

Sergei freezes. "We just wanted whatever money you had."

Sure they did. The blow from that pry bar would have killed me.

"We... We—" His words failing him, Sergei sits back onto the ground and holds both his hands up toward me, as if to show me they are empty and that he poses no further threat. "Don't shoot," he says softly. "Please don't kill me."

He looks pathetic pleading for his miserable life, but I doubt this is a life either he or Anatoli chose. Gorelov and I may be the victims of their attack, but they are the victims of a society that has failed them.

"Luck is with you today," I say, backing toward the corridor.

Gorelov slides around Sergei and joins me.

"If either of you ever cross my path again, your luck will be up."

Sergei doesn't move. He covers his bowed head with his arms.

We quickly make our way to the front of the tenement, but I stop Gorelov from exiting onto the street. I peek out. The cloud pack above Aurestapol's skyline has just started to lighten. The smell of coal smoke is heavy on the cold, gray air. The city is just beginning to stir, and for now the street is quiet.

"Do you have a fountain pen?" I ask Gorelov. "A fountain pen," I repeat when he gapes at me dumbfoundedly.

Gorleov reaches beneath his coat and removes a black pen. He extends it to me, confusion etching his features.

"This will only take a moment." I holster my FP and make a circle motion with my index finger. Gorelov understands and turns his back to me. I place the onionskin sheet between his shoulder blades and write an address on the paper.

I give the pen back to Gorelov, and he absent-mindedly returns it to his pocket.

"Almost done." I tear the sheet in half and stuff the typed orders back into my pocket. I fan the other half until the ink is dry and then fold it into a crude paper glider.

"What—"

I check his question with an upraised finger. I lean out the doorway of the tenement and throw the glider into the air. It rises quickly into the sky where it catches the air currents and is whisked off over the top of the tenement.

"Now we can go," I say.

Gorelov watches the glider disappear. "Go where?"

"First, breakfast, and then I'm going to get you to Ordinburg."

For several minutes, we travel south without incident, but even sticking to the alleyways and small side streets, we can't avoid all encounters. Luck is with us, however; the two Red Cuffs posted at the corner are looking the other way when I poke my head out of the alley. We circle back and give them a two-block berth, then use a crossing trolleybus for cover.

After half an hour of brisk walking, we come into a neighborhood of old slat-board walk-ups fronted by small shops. At this hour, the shops are still shuttered, but the lights of a few are on as the proprietors arrange shelves and dusty counters. Two old men in rough woolen coats crowd a food stall as the vendor rolls back the front, allowing a pleasant, oily smell to tumble across the sidewalk. A teen sweeping the stoop of a general mercantile casually notes our passing with a nod before he turns back to his labor.

At my side, Gorelov's breathing is labored, so I force myself to slow the pace. I don't know what he does for the Ministry of Ethics and Culture, but I suspect he doesn't do anything more physical than shift stacks of papers. I doubt he's ever been forced to run for his life. In some ways, I envy him his old life, and I feel guilty that I have had a hand in him losing it.

"How much farther?" Gorelov asks, his face red from more than the exertion. "My ears are getting frostbite." Without his hat, Gorelov's bald head must be bleeding heat.

Fortunately, our destination is near. We turn down a side street, putting the wind at our back. My cheeks suddenly burn in the relative warmth. Two blocks down we come to a small tearoom run by an elderly lady named Iskara. I peer through the window fronting the street; the place is empty except for the old proprietor sitting on a stool near the back knitting.

"A teashop?" Gorelov says in disbelief.

"Better than a Red Cuff interrogation room," I say, giving him a facile smile.

"You said—"

A withering glare cows him into silence.

Iskara looks up as the opening door strikes a small bell hung from the ceiling. I nod a greeting at her as she rises and motions toward a table near the front. I point instead to a round table in the back and she sweeps her hand in that direction.

I slide one of the chairs around so I can look out the front window at the people passing on the street. Gorelov collapses thankfully into the other chair without bothering to unbutton his coat. The table is covered with a delicate cloth, fringed with lace. A tea stain in the middle peeks out from under a vase of dried flowers. The place is much how I remember it, although a bit old and a bit shabbier.

We wait quietly for Iskara to finish setting out cups and saucers and a small platter of thin pancakes, bowls of assorted jams, sugar, honey, and condensed milk. Iskara's smile is friendly but generic. I'm not sure she recognizes me. I used to frequent this place many years ago. It was a quiet sanctuary from my hectic life, but more importantly, it was a piece of normalcy that others took for granted, but growing up in a state orphanage, I never had. I stopped coming after I returned from a mission to El Emir that had gone wrong in many ways and reinforced that my life had, and would, never be normal. Sitting in here now, I realize that was a mistake.

When she retreats to the samovar in the back corner to draw our tea, Gorelov leans closer to me and whispers hoarsely, "You said you'd get me to Ordinburg."

"There are other things to do first."

"What other things?"

"Stay alive, for one."

Gorelov nervously wipes his brow with his napkin.

I'd like to tell him I've got everything under control, but I don't. I can sense things derailing. If Katalin hasn't done so already, it's only a matter of time before she learns of Mélon's failure and becomes the third entity searching for us. She may even learn about my presence in Aurestapol, and given her apparent double agent status, all three groups could then know I'm here. That means I don't have much time left to accomplish what I had originally come to Aurestapol to do. All I seem to be doing is acquiring complications.

Iskara returns bearing to two pots. She knots her

hands together. The knuckles are swollen from arthritis, but they don't seem to dampen her friendly smile. "Is there anything else I can bring you, Mr. Petrenko? Perhaps some cheese?"

Her recognition surprises me, but then she was always a friendly woman who believed her job entailed more than just brewing and serving tea.

"No, but thank you, Iskara Sergeevna." Her kindness toward me, as much as her excellent tea, always brought me back to her shop.

Gorelov frowns as he checks his engraved pocket watch. He exhales loudly and stuffs it back into his coat.

"Have some tea, Mr. Gorelov."

"How does this get me to Ordinburg, *Mr. Petrenko?*"

I do my best to ignore the implications of his tone; I had been clear the name I gave him was one of several aliases. "It will." I spread strawberry jam on a pancake, hoping it hides my uncertainty.

Resigned, Gorelov fills his cup with tea from the small pot and dilutes it with water from the larger. I follow, adding a slice of lemon. The tea's smoky aroma is pleasant and rich. Its warmth will be a welcome balm to my sore body. Gorelov sighs again after his first sip, but this time he sounds more content.

We say nothing for another twenty minutes.

Nervous, I check my own pocket watch then return to watching the street.

Gorelov loosens his coat, which I take as good sign. He starts to say something but stops mid-sound. A second attempt also fails, leaving him staring down into his tea cup. A minute later, Gorelov manages to organize his thoughts and finally asks, "This all goes back to that investigation of Counter Affairs?"

I nod as I sip my tea.

"But that was years ago. A decade at least. Why—" Frowning, he shakes his head.

"Tell me about the investigation?"

Gorelov's pale lips tighten into a thin line. He looks a little ashen overall, but I'm not sure exactly what that means, especially given his situation.

"It was a routine investigation," he says.

I doubt that immediately.

As he tells me this, Gorelov stares me in the eyes without moving. People think liars break eye contact when plying their trade. That's true for people not accustomed to telling lies, but people who see lots of inexperienced lying know the common behavioral tells, and good liars are students of the craft. My entire life is a web of intricate falsehoods, and one of the most important things I learned when I joined The Order was the value of a convincing lie, and by extension, how to identify one. People who lie for a living either get good at it, or they don't make much of a living, or in my case, wind up dead. While I suspect Gorelov has had to hide the truth many times in his career as an investigator, I suspect he is no longer accustomed to lying.

Besides, even if Gorelov isn't overcompensating with his intent eye contact, nothing related to The Order is ever routine, even for the Inspector General's office. I decide to fish for a real answer. "You were looking at chain of command because the Emperor was concerned about loyalty," I say, forcing the bluff to sound like a statement of fact.

Gorelov's jaw tightens, a nearly involuntary

clenching that tells me I'm right. He eats some jam directly from his spoon in an effort to cover. "It was routine," he says, stirring his tea with the same spoon.

I think back to that time. I was a new recruit, fresh out of my training when the investigation was underway. I know that, because Odella, who had worked as a clerk on the investigation, told me about it several months ago when Lera and I had been forced to seek refuge at her family manor outside of Aurestapol. My stomach turns sour at the memory of that visit—too many surprises—but I push the memory of that encounter away because I can't let it distract me.

Gorelov stares down into his tea, his forehead crinkled into a half-dozen deep fissures. He has stopped stirring his tea, but he continues to hold the spoon in the cup.

"You work for Counter Affairs, yes?"

"But as I said, I—"

"I'm not interested in your personal troubles right now," Gorelov says coldly.

Fair enough.

He continues, "As someone who works for Counter Affairs, I know you have...resources at your disposal that most do not have?"

I nod, sensing where he is going. "I am your best chance to get back..." My voice trails off because my focus narrows on the person standing on the other side of the street. "Stay here," I say, getting to my feet. Gorelov moves to follow me, but I tell him again to stay where he is.

As I stand, Iskara rises from her knitting.

"Could you bring us more hot water?" We don't need hot water, but she needs something to do.

"Who is that?" Gorelov asks, following my line of sight.

"Help." Or at least that's what I hope it is.

The person on the other side of the street doesn't leave when I come out and cross.

"I guess I shouldn't be surprised it's you," Birdie says. She wears the same cloak she had been wearing when I last saw her in Olesk. On the back is embroidered an owl with outstretched wings. The way her hood now sits on her head, it obscures the top part of her face and her pointed chin reminds me of an owl's beak. "You look like something they dredged from the bottom of the harbor," she says.

"Good to see you, too."

The corner of her mouth ticks up. She hands me a scrap of creased onionskin. "You shouldn't litter," she says.

I take the paper and stuff it into my pocket without looking at it. Birdie is part of The Order, and like the rest of us, she has a special Talent that makes her good at what she does. Like any Talent, I can't explain how or why hers works, but she attracts information like a ripe melon attracts flies. She has a knack for being at the right table to overhear a snippet of conversation, passing the right park bench where a train ticket has been carelessly left, or getting hit by a wayward paper glider on which someone has scrawled the address of a local teashop.

I've known Birdie almost from my first day in the Order. But while we did our initial training together, and our paths have occasionally crossed since those early years, I don't really *know* her. But that's the best anyone can know someone in The Order, and after what she and Lera did for me in Coruşu, I not only trust that she doesn't want to see me dead, but I also owe her, which makes what I am about to ask doubly difficult.

"I heard you were in town," she says.

"Where did you hear that?"

She smiles at me inscrutably. "A lady never tells," she says, which draws a smile from me. "I heard you were up north somewhere. In hiding."

"Something like that," I say.

"After Coruşu, I wouldn't blame you." Birdie's breath mists around her head, shimmering in the morning light. Even though the street is empty, I feel exposed to prying eyes and listening ears, but I know that I can't go anywhere more private. I don't want to ask her into the tearoom just yet, and I can't let the tearoom door out of my sight, so I'm resigned to stand in the cold.

"About that," I say. "Why did you come to find me?"

Birdie tries to shrug me off. "You'd have done the same for me."

I'd like to think that's true, but I'm not so sure, especially if R had told me not to go, like she had apparently told Birdie. But R isn't Birdie's handler, so maybe she doesn't carry the same influence. Did Birdie's handler know? That's an intriguing question, and one that might illuminate how systemic my betrayal was within The Order.

"Who else knows you came to Coruşu?" I ask.

"If I had known this was going to be an interrogation, I would have brought a lamp. If you don't trust me, why did you invite me here?"

"I do trust you. You risked a lot to help me in Coruşu, and it wasn't simply because I'm a nice guy.

You don't know me well enough to know if I am or not."

Birdie exhales. "Lera is right; you're an ass, but I do know you're a good agent and loyal to the Empire. We can't afford to waste people like you. Not now."

"You don't believe I've gone rogue."

"I believe you think you have a very good reason to be doing what you're doing."

"That isn't a straight answer," I say.

"No, it's not, but going rogue doesn't mean you're a traitor, either. I'm sure there is a good reason you're in hiding from...well...everyone, it would seem. That reason, I suspect, is whatever you learned in Coruşu." When I don't respond, Birdie gets more direct. "What happened in Coruşu?"

I consider my answer carefully. I have already decided I trust her enough to help me with Gorelov; I should trust her with this information, too. Under the old rules, I would never do that—the less she knew, the less she could give away, intentionally or otherwise—but as R said, maybe it's time to start playing by new rules. I smooth my scraggly beard. How much do I tell her? My head is full of so much information, all of which I am sure is linked together, but I just don't know how the pieces fit.

"Don't hold out on me now, Calypto. You brought me here, remember?"

I take a deep breath. Birdie's concerned expression gives me the strength to continue. "I wasn't meant to come back from Coruşu. I was set up."

"Who?"

My answer sticks in my throat, but I manage to croak it out. "The Order."

"Don't razz me, Calypto."

"That's R's assessment, and I've got to admit, I believe it. A woman calling herself Katalin Kovac and posing as a Red Cuff, was behind it. She's one of ours."

"Are you sure?" Birdie cannot hide the disbelief in her voice.

"Based on a reliable source. I'm sure."

Birdie paces as she struggles to wrap her head around this information. She stops suddenly. "This can't be right. It doesn't add."

"No, it doesn't. But that's not all. The Silver Tigers aren't revolutionaries. It's complicated, but they're after something...bigger."

"Bigger?" Like I did in Coruşu, Birdie is having a hard time seeing what could be bigger than the Empire, and I can't fault her difficulty. We are indoctrinated to believe in and fight for the Empire and all its structure, but if Dai Li is to be believed, there is something in the Empire that transcends it.

"They're after The Order," I say.

A nervous laugh bubbles forth from Birdie. "I told you not to razz me."

"I'm not." I say the words slowly, with deadly seriousness. "That's what I was told in Coruşu by a Silver Tiger that I know as Dai Li."

Birdie's eyes narrow. I sense her question before she has a chance to ask it.

"I don't know if I believe it or not. Question everything, right? She said The Order transcended our boundaries and that it doesn't answer to the Emperor. The Silver Tigers want to bring down The Order because they think it's a threat."

"That's ridiculous," Birdie says.

"I find this 'ridiculous' idea easier to believe after

recent events. Something is happening in The Order. It has been infiltrated or betrayed or something, but my mission in Coruşu was a set-up."

"Then why aren't you dead?" Birdie asks.

"The Silver Tigers helped me escape."

"The Silver Tigers? I'm confused."

Of course she is. What is old news to me, Birdie has never heard before. I don't have time to explain everything I know in detail, but I feel compelled to tell Birdie more. If nothing else, maybe her talent can provide some illumination. Or maybe I just need to tell all this to *someone*. "Dai Li told me the Silver Tigers have fragmented ideologically. One faction, led by someone called Valentin, is determined to destroy The Order by killing everyone associated with it—like Alexander Olstevski, the government official that was assassinated the morning I left to meet you in Olesk."

"Olstevski?" Birdie's brow crinkles.

"What have you heard?" I ask.

"What have *you* heard?"

We stare at each other for a long moment, neither of us willing to speak first. Finally, I acquiesce.

"I'm certain now that Olstevski was linked to The Order. When I asked R about him, she became defensive and told me to forget the name. Putting it all together, I can only conclude he must be associated with The Order, even if I don't know how."

Birdie nods, and I know we are the same page.

"Your turn," I say.

Birdie's lips press together into a line. "I didn't know what to make of it when I heard it, but now I'm intrigued and more concerned. I think I told you in Olsek that Olstevski was a low-ranking bureaucrat.

I'm not so sure anymore. I heard he was heading to
Sovetsky Airfield to catch an airship the morning he
was killed. Although there are a lot of opinions as to
where he was headed, one constant has been that his
airship wasn't military."

It's my turn to frown. Only the military uses
Sovetsky Field. It is the heart and head of the
Emperor's army, the center from which all our war
strategy originates, and every troop deployment, ship
movement, and air mission is coordinated. It is also
one of the most secure locations in the world. A
civilian such as Olstevski would have needed
clearance from the head of command to even get
within a kilometer of the gate, an approval that is well
above the rank of a minor government bureaucrat. I
don't know what it would take to get clearance to
land an airship there; approval from the top levels of
the government?

"I think he was heading out of the country," Birdie
says. "I have no proof, so call it a gut feeling."

I file away this piece of information for later
because I am not sure what to make of it, and I'm
even less sure how much time we have. "The other
faction doesn't seem to want to kill everyone in The
Order," I continue, getting back to my original
explanation. "In fact, before she died, Dai Li seemed
more interested in recruiting me."

"She's dead?"

A lump rises in my throat. "Krauss shot her."

Birdie makes an obscene noise when I say Krauss's
name.

I can't bring myself to admit the full
circumstances. I'd been forced to leave Dai Li behind
in the tunnels beneath Coruşu, something I've

108

regretted many times since. She could have answered my questions, but it was more than that. She helped me escape a massacre in Olsek. I owe her my life, and now I will never get the chance to repay that debt.

Birdie places her hand on my arm.

Reflexively, I pull away. "How's Lera?" I ask, wanting to navigate away from this subject.

"I haven't seen her since Coruşu," Birdie says. "I haven't heard anything, either, so I assume she's fine. They were on the break between Pushkov's camp and the first classroom sessions when we went to Coruşu, so I don't think anyone knows she went."

I still remember that break. I had spent it alone in my apartment, trying to decide whether to spend the money they had given me on a train ticket out of town. Pushkov was notorious for physically breaking down recruits with his regimen of brutal endurance and combat exercises. He took pleasure in two things: hearing recruits curse his name as they sat for hours in freezing cold mud, and then hearing those same recruits thank him years later when what he had taught them had saved their lives. In the end, I didn't leave because I knew deep down that The Order was where I belonged. Looking back, I've often thought that break was intended to test my commitment.

"They still meet at that old ironworks?" I ask.

Birdie grimaces, likely at the memory of the drafty, cavernous building where we sat on wooden stools as a procession of nameless instructors pounded all manner of information and skills into our heads. "I heard they have a new place above a bakery or something," she says. "It's a block south of the Underneath. Remember that place?"

I shrug noncommittally, but I do remember the

Underneath. It had been a popular club then, frequented by young bourgeois, both government and civilian. I had met Odella there. And I had left her there. I looked down at my shoes and the conversation lulls for several awkward seconds. It's time to move past the pleasantries.

"I need your help" I say. "Two things, actually."

"And I thought you just wanted to stroll down memory lane."

"I need to get a message to someone outside of Ordinburg this morning. Do you have any contacts there you trust and that can be discreet?"

"Today? Hmm. I can't make any promises, but I might know someone who can help you. What's the second thing?"

"I need to get someone to Ordinburg as quickly, and as quietly, as possible."

"How quietly?"

"We've been dodging Red Cuff patrols all night."

Birdie makes a clicking sound with her tongue. "So you're the reason for Red Cuff twins at every other intersection. I don't know; this is a big ask."

I grunt acknowledgement. "And I already owe you one too."

"You're right; you do." She grins at me, but she has every right to say that. Nonetheless, her words rub me like sand in my shoes. I didn't ask her to come to Coruşu. She came of her own volition. Yet, it's for that reason I trust she will not betray me now. That may prove to be foolish sentiment, but I hope that concern is unwarranted.

"Can you help or not?" My tone is testier than I intend.

Birdie's lips push together and her gaze burns. She

draws a restrained breath. "The Red Cuffs will be all over Grand Station," she says, "but I might know of a lorry going to Tver, and the Tver station might not be so...infested."

Tver is modest-sized town about an hour northwest of Aurestapol. It's on the main line that runs to Ordinburg. If the Red Cuffs haven't learned about the whereabouts of Gorelov's wife yet, it's doubtful they would have a presence at that station.

"I'll need some time to arrange it. Can you lie low until—"

"About that," I say.

Birdie throws up her arms. "*Oy!*"

"I didn't plan this," I say. "I'm here for...other business that I need to wrap up today. Aurestapol isn't exactly the safest place for me right now."

"It's getting more dangerous by the second."

"I'm sorry to put you in a tough spot. I didn't know who else to ask. I'm a little short of allies at the moment."

"What's this business of yours?"

I feel like I've already said too much. "It's safer if you don't know."

"You don't get to play that card," Birdie says.

I rub at the scruff on my chin, weighing my options. I trust Birdie as much as I can trust anyone under the circumstances, otherwise I would not have sought her, but if Katalin Kovac or Krauss learns Birdie has talked with me, or even learns about what she did in Corușu, she would become a target. The less she knows, the better for her. And for me.

Birdie starts to turn it away. "Have it your way."

"Wait."

She looks at me expectantly.

"After everything I've already told you, you're still interested in helping me?"

"That's just it. After everything you've told me, I have little choice; the fate of the Empire could hang on this, but you either tell me everything, or we're done here because I'm not going to play with half a deck. That's how we all lose."

She's right. I've brought her into this mystery, and I'm asking a lot of her. She deserves to know everything. In addition, should anything happen to me, at least one other person will know what I know, and that could be critical to the safety of the Empire.

"I recovered something in Coruşu," I say. "I don't know how it fits into all this, but I know it's important."

"That briefcase?"

"Did you open it?"

"Phhh!" She crosses her arms and looks offended.

"Of course you did. I would have."

She shrugs at me. "The fancy egg thing?"

I nod, deciding not to tell her about the phial of sand I found hidden inside; old habits are tough to shake. "It's got to be a clue, but I can't figure it out, so I'm trying to find someone who can tell me something—anything—about it."

Birdie studies me as if trying to figure out if I've told her everything. She uncrosses her arms. "Who is this person you need to move?"

I exhale, not realizing I had been holding my breath. I don't know what I would have done if she had walked away. "His name is Anton Gorelov. He's with the Ministry of Ethics and Culture now, but previously he was with the Inspector General. Ten year ago, he was involved in an investigation of The

Order by that office. People have taken an interest in whatever he learned during that investigation." As I talk, I start across the street, and Birdie takes the cue and follows. "He promised to answer my questions about the investigation if I got him back to his family in Ordinburg."

"Before the Red Cuffs," Birdie says, immediately understanding the situation.

"Given everything, I don't have the time to properly cultivate a relationship with him."

As we reach the other side of the street, Birdie grabs my arm. "How important is he?"

I know the answer immediately, but I hesitate nonetheless given what it may mean for Gorelov and his family.

Birdie arches an expectant eyebrow.

"Class A," I say. "He's in here." I open the door to Iskara's tearoom and follow Birdie inside.

My throat tightens.

The tea pots and cups and little plates of food are still on the table in the back of the room, but Gorelov's chair is empty.

"Wha—"

At my surprised sound, Iskara looks up from her knitting needles.

I had watched the only door into the tearoom carefully. No one had come in or gone out.

Iskara nods toward a brightly painted blue door in the back corner. The toilet. Of course.

I hand Birdie a few bills and motion toward Iskara. While she pays, I rap lightly on the wooden door. "Anton Gorelov, it's time to go."

No reply.

"Gorelov?"

The door isn't locked and the cramped, dingy toilet is empty and cold. High on the back wall, the narrow window is open. It's small, but with some effort, Gorelov's slender frame could have squeezed through it.

I loose a curse.

I climb up onto the back of the toilet and look out into the empty back alley.

"He's gone," I say, coming back into the tearoom. I cut off another string of curses before they can bubble up. I didn't think there was another way out of the tearoom—I've never used the toilet here and never thought it would have a window, let alone one through which Gorelov could fit.

I shake my head. With even five minutes' head start, he could be anywhere right now, assuming he got very far at all; he's probably already been picked by the Red Cuffs.

"Now what?" Birdie asks, as we stand outside the tearoom. The clouds overhead are packed tighter than ever, and it feels like a freezing rain is about to open up on us.

I scuff the toe of my boot on the sidewalk in frustration. "He's trying to get to his family. That's the only lead I've got." On the albeit slim chance he can avoid the Red Cuffs and the Silver Tigers and whatever other person Katalin Kovac sends after him, I could try to beat him to Ordinburg and intercept him. That would mean abandoning my mission in Aurestapol; perhaps even leaving behind the phial of sand. I dismiss that thought immediately. R always said to finish the mission. "My other work here is more important," I say.

"I'll reach out to some contacts," Birdie says.

"Maybe they will have heard something."

It won't be good news, but I don't voice the thought. I've yet to get any good news since arriving in Aurestapol.

"What about your message?"

"There is no reason to send it anymore," I say. I don't know where Gorelov's in-laws live, or even their family name. I could dig it up, sure, but at what cost in time, and by then it would probably be worthless. Once I figured out where to send it, either Gorelov will have already sent warning, or he will have been picked up, rendering any threat to his wife and son impotent.

"I'm going to wrap things up today." I pull up the collar of my long coat and adjust my hat. "There's a small park a block east of St. Vladimir's Church," I say. "It has several stone tables and benches that are popular in the summer with old men who like to play chess. Do you know it?"

"No, but I can find it."

"Let's meet there at sunset."

Birdie's eyes narrow. "Don't be late."

PART III

PATH INTO SHADOW

Time is an agent's enemy. Too little or too much can be equally disastrous, although I tend to think too much time is worse—idle hands and all that. I suspect the person who coined the phrase "killing time" had greater insight than most give credit.

Professor Voynov isn't expecting me until this afternoon, and given all that has happened, I should not be on the street. I should find an out-of-the-way place to pass the time in warmth and anonymity. Iskara's tearoom would have been perfect, but if Gorelov has fallen into enemy hands as I suspect, he could tell them about her. I don't want to bring any additional trouble onto Iskara by being there when a squad of Red Cuffs or a Silver Tiger assassin shows up to investigate. Given no provocation, I expect they would leave an old woman alone.

Against my better judgment, I search the nearby streets for Gorelov. I come across a pair of Red Cuffs in *pilokas* going shop to shop, and I lower my face as I pass on the other side of the road. For now, Gorelov appears to have evaded the Red Cuffs, but they're only a part of the danger he faces. Yet, if he managed to elude them, maybe he can slip past the Silver Tigers and The Order too, but the question is for how long?

I go by his house on the chance he's naïve enough to return there. A pair of Red Cuffs stands on the front stoop talking. The front door is open behind them, and as I casually walk past on the opposite side of the street, I see a jumble of furniture piled in the hallway and at the bottom of the stairs. Enough people are on the street heading to work now, that my presence isn't noteworthy, but I take care not to slow too much or to gawk too openly.

I'm nearly past the front door, and about to turn my attention forward again, when the Red Cuff on the stoop with his back to me turns. My stomach lurches painfully, and for a dreadful moment, I am nearly sick. Krauss scans the street as he sets his lighter to a cigarette pinched between his thin lips.

My entire body starts to shake. Reflexively I reach for the FP under my long coat, but instead I force my hand to flip up the collar of my coat so as not to draw suspicion. Keep walking, I tell myself.

Krauss exits Gorelov's wrought iron gate and turns in the same direction that I am traveling. He falls into step a few meters behind me, where I cannot see him in my peripheral vision. Even though he is on the opposite side of the street, I feel his menace like a black bubble pushed before him.

I find it hard to draw a breath.

The last time I encountered Krauss, he nearly killed me. If not for Katalin Kovac, he would have; of that I am sure. She would not allow him kill me without first extracting a confession to treason, and had I not escaped when I did, I might have given them both what they wanted. Yet Krauss did not waste his opportunity. Unable to obtain ultimate satisfaction, he took solace in extracting vengeance in allotments of blood and pain. The scars on my wrists from the sharp metal shackles still ache as a reminder of his cruelty.

My hand gravitates once again toward my FP, but I fight the urge to draw it. The open street is no place for revenge, but revenge is what I will have.

I slow my pace, allowing Krauss to move ahead of me so I can more easily follow him. He pays me no attention; likely he has no idea I am in Aurestapol, and he thinks I am simply another citizen beneath his notice. I allow him to get several meters ahead of me before I match his pace. It is not clear where he is going, but that does not matter. I don't intend to let him to reach his destination.

I cross the street and fall in behind him, careful not to follow too closely. I lower my head so the brim of my hat obscures my face without looking suspicious.

We have come several blocks from Gorelov's door, and the rowhouses have given way to small, dingy shop fronts and walkup apartments whose windows are still rimed with morning frost. With the shops now open, just enough people are on the street to give me some anonymity.

I carefully shift my FP from its shoulder holster to the pocket of my long coat.

Beads of sweat erupt along my forehead, but I barely notice them, as they slide down my temples. I want to make Krauss hurt—that need burns in my belly like a fiery rock of coal. I must make him hurt like he did me in Coruşu, but that means getting him where I can spend time extracting his pain in tortuous measures of flesh. I know I don't have the time for that, so maybe I'll settle for putting a fletchette through his throat and watching the life drain from his eyes. A fast death is too good for him, but it's all the time I have.

Then I am wracked with the realization I am letting emotions override my common sense. That's a short path to catastrophe.

What am I doing?

Confronting Krauss now, here, is needlessly dangerous and serves no purpose.

I slow, allowing Krauss to pull ahead of me.

Each step he takes tears like a knife eviscerating me. I can't let his past deeds go unavenged. I simply cannot. That is the purpose a confrontation serves. It will give me closure on events that have haunted me in the weeks since Coruşu. Just as importantly, it will rid me of future complications.

The street has momentarily cleared of pedestrians and autos, so I push aside the voice in my head pleading for restraint and quickly come up behind Krauss. As he starts to turn, I draw my FP and force it into the side of his left check as I grab him around the neck with my right arm.

"Don't," is all I say as I force him toward a narrow alley between two brick buildings.

He doesn't struggle, but he doesn't come willingly either, so I muscle him into the alley, jerking him around a couple of times to keep him off balance. His face makes a satisfying thud as I push him against the brick wall.

"I'll put a dozen through your face if you so much

as shrug," I say.

"Calypto?" He sounds surprised, not afraid.

I don't respond, but press my weight against his back so I can use my right hand to pat him down and take his FP. I tuck the weapon into my pocket, but don't allow myself to get complacent; Krauss may be unarmed, but he is not weaponless.

"You have more lives than an alley cat," Krauss says, his tone a sneer.

"Maybe we'll find out how many you have."

"Let's not be hasty." A change in his tone; maybe he hears the edge in my voice.

I push my FP harder into his cheek to make my point that I'm serious and dangerous. I want to pull the trigger and tear a hole through his face, but my finger betrays me, and I realize then that I can't bring myself to simply shoot him. As much as he deserves to die for what he did to me—and especially Carlo—in Coruşu, I'm not a cold-blooded killer.

At this moment, I hate myself for that fact.

"I should have shot you when I had the chance," Krauss says. "That's what traitors deserve."

I don't bother to refute him. He's only trying to distract me to get the upper hand, but I won't play into his game. "You were too busy being an obedient lapdog," I say, hoping it will goad him. If he tries to escape, maybe I can justify to myself shooting him.

My barb doesn't have the desired effect, however. Instead, Krauss laughs.

"You can't do it, can you?" he says.

"Shut up." I push his face against the bricks, extracting a satisfying grunt from him as I scrape skin from his nose and forehead.

Krauss mumbles a curse, but doesn't make any

effort to resist me.

I feel like cursing my impetuousness. I should have listened to that little voice of restraint in my head. I've killed people, but I'm not a killer, so what made me think I could execute Krauss in an alleyway? What he did to me in Coruşu should be enough motivation. Coruşu wasn't the first time, either. El Emir had been terrible too, but compared to what he did to me in Coruşu, it had been a visit to the podiatrist. I have every justification to put a dozen fletchettes into Krauss's neck, but my trigger finger's sudden morality paralyzes it. It seems to know better the line such an action will cross. It's a line over which you don't come back.

"You're gutless," Krauss says.

"Who says I ever intended to kill you?" I hope I've delivered it with sufficient bravado to hide the fact it's a lie. My mind churns through scenarios. I can't stand here all day holding him against the brick wall, and tying him up like I did with Mélon is not a viable option at this point. If I don't shoot him, my only other choice is to let him go.

Maybe I can turn that to my advantage.

"I'm going to share some information with you," I say, "one patriot to another."

"You're no—" Krauss goes quiet as the tip of my pistol digs deeper into his cheek. I'll have to settle for the satisfaction that I'll leave a bruise on his face that he won't be able to easily explain.

"All you have to do is shut up and listen. Understand?"

Krauss starts to say something, but stops and instead dips his head in a shallow nod.

"Your partner in Coruşu—"

"Kovac?"

"What did I say? Ears open; mouth shut."

I give him an opportunity to respond, but he shows me my message has been received. I ease back on my pistol to acknowledge his silence.

"Kovac isn't what she appears to be," I say. "She's playing you to get her dirty work done."

"I don't believe you." Krauss blurts the words, as if he can't control himself, so I overlook the infraction.

"I'm not asking you believe me. I'm giving you a warning, and what you choose to do with that is your business. Keep your eyes open because people aren't always what they appear to be."

"Like you."

"Exactly like me." I drive my knee into the back of his right thigh, and he screams out as his leg buckles. With my left hand I drive him down into the pavement. Krauss's shoulder crunches, and he immediately grabs it and curls into a ball. He spits curses about my parentage between his clenched teeth. I've dislocated his arm, and if fortune is with me, I've broken his clavicle.

As I step around him, I notice his flask has fallen out of his pocket. He had taunted me with that flask in Coruşu. As long as I've known him, he's had it. In El Emir he told me it had been his father's. I don't know why I remember that, and I'm not even sure it's true. It doesn't matter if it is or not—he values it, and that's exactly why I take it.

I make a point of showing him I have it before I slip into an inside pocket of my long coat where it will be safe. "For the next time I'm with friends," I say.

Krauss tries to grab my pants leg and recoils in pain.

I leave him in the alleyway and start down the street at a fast walk. I put a half-dozen blocks between us before I slow. My shirt clings to my back, and I grow chilled now as the adrenaline flushes from my system.

I know I will regret not having killed him, but I think I've given Krauss something that will torment him for a long time, and which, I hope, will pay future dividends. It was obvious in Coruşu he resented Katalin Kovac, or at least her authority over him. Whether Krauss believes me or not, I have now sown a seed of doubt that I'm reasonably certain will blossom with time.

A smile perks up the corners of my mouth.

At the first opportunity, I remove the cartridge from Krauss's FP and surreptitiously dump the weapon into a garbage bin.

I check my pocket watch. It's still too early to return to the university, but I had hoped to do one more thing before meeting with Professor Voynov again. I turn south on the next major thoroughfare and walk for twenty minutes until I'm in a familiar neighborhood of cramped apartments, quaint hundred-year-old shops and smoky basement bars. I lived not far from here when I first joined The Order; they put me in a one-room flat with a dodgy radiator and rotting asbestos floor, but it was nicer than anything I'd ever had, and most importantly, it was *my* place. In the decades since, the neighborhood has changed little, as if time has gotten stuck. Sure, the buildings are a little shabbier, but that can be as a much a product of the gloomy morning and the austerity of these brutal times, as any deficiency of time. All of Aurestapol seems shabbier these days.

Although I know it still exists, I'm surprise when I see the sign for the Underneath. Most bars come and go so quickly, but the Underneath is a local icon that has weathered the fickle trends of the industry. The basement bar has survived nearly a century by appealing to the most primal desires of young people: an abundance of vodka, hearty food, and music to which they can flirt. I met Odella here, a week after moving into the neighborhood, and for those first months I spent evenings spinning my lies to her accompanied by romance songs sung to soulful pianos.

I shake the nostalgia from my thoughts as I pass the steps down to the Underneath. The bar's door looks the same as I remember, although the red paint has dulled. I know it's not possible, but I would give much to be able to step through that door and go back ten years. I'd fix everything.

But time moves immutably forward.

I pause at the next corner and check the shops in each direction. Birdie mentioned The Order's new training area was above a bakery south of the Underneath. If my memory has not entirely failed, Kastonov's used to be around here. Then I see its small, soot-darkened sign about block down the narrow side street.

I'm taking a risk coming here, but I'm gambling that no one will recognize me. I've met few people in The Order—that I am aware of, at least—and other than a handful of field agents whose paths I've crossed in my years, I doubt I would recognize many of them if we bumped chests on the street. I am confident the same would be true for them. That doesn't mean I should be careless, so I loiter on the corner, trying not to look like a rapscallion sizing up potential marks. An old woman with a cane clicks-clicks a wide path around me, giving evidence I'm failing.

Certainly, I look the rascal part: locs tangled after a night sleeping on a hard floor, and beard getting even more feral with each passing day; even my long coat is looking weary-worn with new tears in the sleeve and shoulder. Fortunately, its dark color masks the blood.

Twenty minutes pass.

A drink of vodka from Krauss's flask warms me temporarily, but another twenty minutes go by. Maybe Birdie heard it wrong? Even she admits that not every rumor she hears is true.

I check my pocket watch and decide to give it five more minutes. My hands are getting numb because I don't have any gloves.

I'm about to leave when movement down the block catches my attention. Two people bundled in coats come out of the door next to the bakery. They part and the man, head lowered, starts down the street away from me. The other turns in my direction. She's tiny, the top of her head would barely come to my shoulder. Her scarf is piled thickly around her neck, covering most of her face and hair. Thick glasses peer over the top of the scarf—not so much glasses as aviator goggles, held on by a thick strap running around the back of her head.

As she turns in my direction, I start to walk, paralleling her on the opposite side of the street so I can watch. After a block, I see no one following her and cross at the next intersection to wait. She doesn't notice me as she comes to the corner. I'm not sure if she just doesn't recognize me or if she doesn't see me. Lera is blind. Sort of blind, actually. Her vision does not work through air. She can only see through water, and the water-filled goggles she wears create lenses that give her only rudimentary sight, at best. I don't know the boundaries of her Talent, but I have learned two things related to it. First, if used carelessly, her Talent would likely destroy her, and second, she doesn't like to talk about it. I've witnessed both of these firsthand.

"Not even a hello, Lera?"

She turns toward me. A strand of her dark hair falls down over one of her goggle eyepieces. Through the water lenses, her eyes are large, white orbs. They have no irises, and the pupils are milky white, making them look like pickled pearl onions in a bowl.

"Calypto?" she says through the wall of scarf. "This is a surprise."

"I hope not the bad kind of surprise."

"That's to be determined. What are you doing here?" She does not blink once during this entire time. I had forgotten how disconcerting that is.

Before I can respond, another person joins us on the corner. I had been so focused on Lera I hadn't noticed him until he was standing next to us. He is several centimeters shorter than me and dressed in a smart-cut coat and the latest style of hat. The hair on the sides of his head glistens with hair slick, consistent with the latest style popular among young bourgeois. His rectangular glasses glint in the diffuse daylight as he pushes the wire frames back up onto his nose with a white-gloved finger.

"Is this rascal bothering you, Miss Lera?"

Lera's lips crinkle as she puckers them in what I perceive as annoyance. "Not presently," she says.

Our visitor surveils me from head to foot as if inspecting a suit that's a decade out of fashion. Then he pulls off his white glove and extends his right hand toward me. "I'm Nikolai."

Lera grabs Nikolai's wrist and pulls his hand away from me. "Don't," she says, scowling at him.

"I'm just being friendly," Nikolai says, smiling pleasantly.

It's a fake smile. After years doing what I do, I know a fake one when I see it.

Lera pulls at my elbow, and I go with her, but I don't take my eyes off Nikolai. As we cross the street, Lera glares back at him standing on the corner behind us.

"I don't think he recognized you," she says as we reach the other side of the street.

"Who is he?" I ask.

"He's a real blighter," she says.

I arch an eyebrow.

"He's been demonstrating basic shadowing techniques the past two days. He's all hands, and not in a good way."

"He's with The Order then?"

"I would assume so," she says. "Is he still back there?"

I glance back again and the street corner is empty. "It looks like he's moved on."

"Good. Yesterday he followed me, but I managed to lose him. Creep."

"Perhaps he was testing you."

Lera growls a low rumble of annoyance.

"You want me—"

"I'm handling it," she says sharply.

I hold my hands up in mock surrender. "Okay, I get it. You can take care of yourself."

"At least one of us can."

"Why the hostility?" It's been less than a minute and she's already insulting me as if I'm a contemptable younger sibling, and I've got more than a decade on her.

"That wasn't hostility," she says, although I don't hear any contrition in her voice. "You've caught me by surprise. I didn't know you were back in town."

"The announcement must have gotten lost in the post."

"You're an ass."

I try not grin, but can't stop the corners of my mouth from curling upwards.

We continue down the street. It's only been a few months since I first met Lera in Olesk, but I swear she's grown taller by several centimeters. Then I realize she isn't taller: she's matured. That headstrong but naïve orphan has lost her doe-soft lines. A hardness borne from experience settles onto her features like a brutal winter weathers the façade of a farm house.

A few months learning how to live in the new reality of our world will do that.

The Order changes you; it changes everyone.

I went from a withdrawn, weak, and scared teen to...well, not something I look back on with any pride. Arrogant, certainly, even though I told myself it was self-confidence. Self-absorbed...I was guilty of that, too, and probably I still am. We all handle the new power that The Order gives us differently. I like to think I have grown as a human being, but those early years weren't my finest. One need only to ask Odella if he has misconceptions about that.

With Lera, however, I sense her growth is different. She's strong, but I believe she has always been strong. The set of her shoulders suggests a readiness to face the world almost to the point of rebelliousness. She has not been cowed and humbled by The Order's training. Instead, it looks as if the challenge is curing her into something that will be formidable.

"Why are you here?" she asks, her tone tinged with concern, not accusation. She must understand something about my situation.

"I never had a chance to thank you for Coruşu," I say.

"There wasn't time."

"No, there wasn't."

Lera stops walking, and my stride carries me several steps down the side walk before I, too, can stop. She folds her arms across her breasts and cocks her head to the left. The lenses of her goggles shimmer in the light.

"What?" I ask.

She passes me and keeps going down the street. "Never mind."

I hustle to catch up with her.

"Nothing," she says again, which means it's something. Maybe she hasn't matured as much as I thought. She stops walking then and folds her arms again. She takes a step away from me, as if she wants to establish some minimum distance between us. "Some folks have said you've gone rogue or worse, turned."

I bite off my initial response, making only a stuttering sound. I take a deep breath to calm myself. Anyone who would think that doesn't know me, and in truth, I don't really care what those people think.

"What do you think?" I ask Lera.

"A lot of people are stupid is what I think," Lera says. "I'm just telling you what people are saying." She continues when my eyebrows press together in confusion. "It's not like I've received an official communique—that's not how it works. I heard Petrov say something the other day. One of the other recruits, too. Rumors. But rumors come from somewhere, yes?"

"I haven't turned," I say. "My loyalties are and have always been true to the Empire."

"You don't have to tell me that," Lera says.

To be honest, I didn't think I did. Yet it's good to hear her reaffirm this.

"This is about whatever was in that case? The one from Coruşu? People in your condition don't hold on to something that tightly unless it's very important."

"You didn't—"

"No, didn't open it. Birdie wouldn't let me. Wasn't the mission, blah, blah. She can be a real liability at times."

I can't contain the grin sliding across my lips, but I'm not sure Lera can see it. "Don't let Birdie hear you say that."

Lera shrugs. "So, what was in that case that you nearly got yourself killed for?"

"It's more complicated than that."

"Hmph. If you want me to help, you need to start treating me like you trust me."

"That's quite a leap in logic," I say. "Who says I'm

here to recruit you?"

"If you didn't need my help, you wouldn't be talking to me for one of two reasons—" She ticks the two items off on her fingers as she says them. "You *don't* trust me and thus would be afraid I'd turn you in, or you *do* trust me, but you don't want to risk pulling me into this deep mess you've gotten yourself in."

Her big, milky eyes stare up at me. She smiles smugly at her clever logic, seemingly obtuse to other possible options.

One thing she is right about, however, is that finding her is risky, and not just for me. Finding her risks pulling her into the mess I've fallen into. I thought I could mitigate my danger to her—if no one knows I'm in Aurestapol and no one knows we've met, then no harm—but I suddenly have my doubts. Another poor decision, and I've put Lera into jeopardy, and for what?

"I—"

But we both start speaking at the same time, and then we both stop. Lera's gaze never leaves my face, but mine drops to the ground. In that awkward span of silence, I realize I haven't done what I came here to do. I have yet to actually thank her.

"I'm an ass," I say, breaking the chill. "What you and Birdie did for me in Coruşu, I can never repay. Thank you."

"As I see it, we're even. You don't owe me anything."

She's wrong. By my tally, she has saved my life twice. That she also happened to be a beneficiary the first time in Korelov Park doesn't matter. She had risked her sanity, maybe even her life, when she used her Talent on that rainy night. Then she did it again in Coruşu when she didn't need to be there, when she probably should not have been there. No, I owe her more than I could likely ever pay back.

"When are you going to get on the level with me?" Lera asks. "I'm not some fragile flower that needs protecting anymore, and you don't have enough friends to be turning away people who want to help you."

"You're awful eager." In my profession, that's not always a desirable trait, even in a new recruit. Being too eager tends to raise suspicions. I want to lecture her in the finer points of helping—like don't offer to help until you've heard the request—but this isn't the place, and I suspect Lera is the not audience.

"If someone doesn't help you, I'll have to fish your half-frozen body out of some river again."

"So you're saying I'm a charity case?"

"Your words, not mine."

I expect her to signal in some way that she is teasing, but the stern set of her mouth and the defiant hands on her hips suggest only seriousness. Having truly completed what I came to do, I'm tempted not to draw Lera any deeper into this, but then I realize that by virtue of her employ, she is already entwined in the matter. She is part of The Order, and whether as part of a wider agency objective or the effort of one or a few, The Order is after me, and whoever is responsible for these rumors of my disloyalty is actively manipulating everyone into finding me. Knowing the identity of that person would be helpful.

"There is something you can do for me," I say.

"I knew it!"

"Can you be my eyes and ears on the inside?"

Her forehead crinkles. "What do you mean?"

"I suspect someone inside The Order is not working in the best interests of the Empire."

"Besides you?" This time she grins, but the remark still irks me.

"As you have eloquently observed, I don't have anyone in The Order I can trust to learn what's truly happening." Of course this isn't true, but that is not the point.

"I can be that person," Lera says.

"This isn't a spy game."

An annoyed look crosses her face again, but after a moment it disappears. "I'll be careful."

"Take no chances. Do you understand that? No chances. It helps no one if you get caught, least of all you. I want you to listen to what's going on around you. Try to find out who's the source of the rumors, but be careful...be very careful. Don't go looking for trouble. This should be an eyes-and-ears mission only."

She nods curtly at me, and I'm convinced she understands.

"Also, don't tell anyone you know me," I continue. "If anyone does know, diminish it all. Deny everything. Put distance between us any way you can. Soon they will match you with a handler to oversee your final training. No matter how much *you* trust that person, and your life will depend on trusting that person, do not tell him anything about me because I don't know if *I* can trust that person."

Gently she takes my left elbow and gives it a reassuring squeeze. "Don't worry," she says, "I'm not that stupid."

This isn't about being stupid; it's about knowing how to play the game such that you don't have to be carried home in a pine box. In that area, she's a novice up against people trained to lie and detect lies. People who specialize in seeing through subterfuge. People who are trained to root out that which is intended to never be found, and when they find it, deal with it using whatever cold, calculated force necessary. Under these conditions, even a well-trained agent is at risk. Yet for some reason, I'm not as worried about sending Lera into that grinder as I rationally should be.

"I better get going," I say, starting to turn away. "I don't want to risk someone recognizing me."

"Calypto..."

I turn back to her.

She adjusts her scarf pile, her milky eyes fixed on me with their unblinking stare. In the morning light, they seem to glow as if radiating an internal fire. "Be careful."

I don't know if she can see the corners of my mouth pull upward ever so slightly. The sentiment is comforting and comes at a time when I need proof of humanity. "You too, Bright Eyes." I turn away and continue down the street.

"Bright Eyes," she calls out behind me. "I like that."

I don't stop walking, and I don't look back until I've gone several blocks. The corner where Lera had been standing is now empty. I know I have put her in danger, but if I hadn't given her something to help me with, I'm confident she would have freelanced, and she's too inexperienced to do that—not against The Order, at least. I can only hope I have given her a task that will keep her out of even greater danger. If I was a betting man, I would put everything on not seeing her again, but fate has a nasty habit of defying the odds. Something tells me our paths will cross again.

A LINE OF STUDENTS DRAINS from the science
building into the overcast afternoon. Most have their
heads lowered; a few whisper epithets of
disappointment. They sound as if they have just come
from an exam, but perhaps the cold dreariness of the
day affects them.

I squeeze through the mass into the atrium. It's
dotted with clusters of smartly dressed young men
talking quietly. In the eastern corridor, several of the
doors are open, leading into faculty offices. In one an
elderly woman wearing thick glasses taps away on a
typewriter while a student fidgets in a chair to the left
of her desk.

I rap lightly on the wood next to the frosted pane
on Voynov's office door.

"Come." Voynov's voice sounds distant through
the glass.

The door knob is cool against my palm, triggering
a shiver of my shoulders.

The office is empty. Voynov's desk is as cluttered
as it was yesterday, and the books have been

restacked in the hardback chair intended for visitors. Yesterday seems a *very* long time ago, and my available evidence—the wear on my body, the encounters, the revelations—all contradict what the calendar tacked on the wall behind the desk tells me.

Lost as I am in contemplation, I am startled when the grayed sheet hanging behind the cluttered desk parts to reveal Voynov. The narrow doorway leads into a back room.

"Mr. Titov, this is a surprise. I was expecting you later."

"I hope I'm not intruding, but I was in the area and thought I would stop in early. Have you any news on my sand?"

"Quite all right," Voynov says, dismissing my sentiment with a nonchalant wave of his hand. "Unfortunately, I have no news for you. I learned this morning that the colleague I mentioned yesterday is away at a symposium, and not expected back until tomorrow. I hope to catch up with him then and show him your sample."

I resist the urge to frown. This is an unfortunate development, but consistent with my luck since arriving in Aurestapol, so I should not be surprised. Yet Professor Voynov's news is disappointing.

The ticking mantel clock reminds me that my time in Aurestapol is quickly running out. Can I wait another day on the chance of learning something more? Will that something more be sufficiently helpful to justify the risks that seem to multiply by the hour? With Gorelov still out there and the Red Cuffs everywhere, I'm not so sure.

"I appreciate your willingness to help," I say, "but I'm afraid I can't wait that long."

Voynov looks as if his stomach has soured on a questionable bowl of borscht. "Oh, but it is only a short delay," he says, offering a feeble grin. When I don't respond, he sighs heavily. "Very well, but I hate when I cannot send a student away with a smile on his face." He motions with a jerk of his head for me to follow him as he turns into the back room and lets the grayed sheet swing back into place behind him.

The back room turns out to be a cramped laboratory slightly narrower than the professor's office. A work bench runs beneath a window on the opposite wall, and wraps under a set of shelves to my right. The shelves are stocked with brown bottles, jars of powdered chemicals, and an exotic assortment of delicate, hand-blown glassware, bulbs, and tubing. Under the shelves, a stack of well-fingered research journals and hand-written notes stretches across the bench surface, almost entirely obscuring it and blocking a red fire bucket that has been pushed to the back against the wall. On the entirety of the counter beneath the window is a contraption of glass cylinders, rubber tubing, and beakers. Nestled in the ring of a metal work stand, a reddish liquid bubbles gentle in a round bottom flask heated from below by an alcohol burner.

Voynov digs through a clutter of test tube racks, notebooks and a variety of metal implements that sit next to the apparatus. "I brought the sand back here to look at it more closely..." His mumbling trails off as he shifts several small jars of chemicals. "I know it is here." He sounds more as if he is trying to assure himself, than me.

This all makes me nervous, and I regret for the moment leaving the phial with him. To do so had been against my instincts, but I didn't have much choice if I was going to learn anything. Short of finding the researcher Voynov recommended at the University at Çavuş in the Sultanate, I had no other options.

To keep calm, I examine the bubbling flask more closely. My schooling did not include science—I barely got the basics of reading and writing at the orphanage—so Voynov's equipment is as foreign to me as a Quin silk loom. After studying it, however, I conclude it is some sort of distillation apparatus, like you might see as part of still for home-brewing *samogon*. My curiosity getting the better of me, I ask Voynov to explain.

"It's a Kjeldahl reaction," he says, pausing his search. "Ha, I forget that you are not one of my students. I am running this chemical reaction on a sample from the Dagestani region to measure the amount of nitrogen in the soil. It is part of a research project, which is very interesting—"

"Forgive me, Professor, but I am short on time."

Voynov quickly turns his frown into a congenial smile. "Yes, I don't want to bore you. I forget that not everyone finds dirt as fascinating as I do." He turns his attention back to his search, but he is interrupted again by a knock on the office door.

"It is probably a student," he says. "Give me a moment." He slips through the curtain to answer the door, leaving me alone in the laboratory.

Once alone, I move over to where Voynov had been sifting through the clutter on the workbench. My nose crinkles at the mess. How does he find anything in this sty? Notebooks and papers piled in teetering stacks, glass dishes, beakers, bottles of chemicals, some still uncorked. I carefully push a few items aside with the tip of my index finger. Under one of the notebooks is a dusting of grayish power on the bench top, and I take special care not to disturb it.

Then I see the phial. It's rolled against the back of the work bench and been partially hidden under the edge of a grimy cloth. I grab it and hold it up. The light coming in through the window shimmers off the sand as it shifts in the cylinder. I exhale loudly, surprised at how much tension had been knotting my shoulders.

I slide the phial into the pocket of my trousers, and for the first time I notice how quiet it is. Voynov had gone to talk with a student, but I hear nothing from his office. The only sound is the gentle bubbling of the flask on the workbench next to me.

My vision narrows as my senses suddenly become heightened.

I reach into my long coat, but before I can grab the handle of my FP, a voice warns me, "I wouldn't do that." To punctuate the suggestion, an FP pressurizes.

I freeze my hand halfway to where I need it to be, and bite back a curse at my sloppiness. I got so distracted retrieving that damned phial I not only got caught off my guard here, but I allowed myself to be followed.

"Put your hands where I can see—slowly! I'm already feeling jumpy; don't make me more so."

I'm sure I've heard that voice before, but no name or face immediately comes to mind. At least it's not Krauss. Or Katalin Kovac.

"No need to do anything rash," I say as I slowly withdraw my hand from within my long coat. I raise both of them up near the brim of my hat. "Professor Voynov, are you okay?"

"He's fine," the speaker says. "Turn around. Slowly, slowly!" The tension in the voice is clear. He either lacks experience doing this type of thing, or he feels inferior in this particular encounter. Either possibility is an exploitable advantage, provided he doesn't get too trigger jumpy and accidentally shoot me in the throat first.

"Stay calm. I'm turning slowly." As I turn, my teeth grind in anger, as much at my sloppiness as at the identity of my assailant.

Nikolai stands just in the doorway, holding an ashen-faced Voynov between us by the collar of the professor's coat. With his other hand, Nikolai points an FP at me. The tip of the weapon quivers, but Nikolai glares with determination.

How could I let this baby-faced whelp get the jump on me? I had taken precautions to identify and shake any tails, but I must have been sloppy because somehow I had missed Nikolai. Lera did say he was teaching her techniques to shadow people, but that's no excuse. I'm better than this. On the street, he genuinely didn't seem to recognize me and that, distracted as I was, must have subconsciously put me off my guard.

"Calypto, yes?" It's plain from his tone the question is rhetorical and any distant hope I harbored that he didn't recognize me is gone.

I ignore Nikolai's question. "Are you okay, professor?"

Voynov stutters something unintelligible. He's shaken but otherwise appears unharmed.

"Why don't you let the professor go? He doesn't

know anything," I say.

"I will," Nikolai says, "but only after you've been secured."

I'd like to tell Voynov that everything will be okay, but to be honest, I don't know. Lera didn't hold Nikolai in high regard, and his twitchy finger concerns me. Who knows what he really wants to do or, more importantly, what he is actually capable of doing.

If our places had been reversed, and I had not known Voynov's role in all this, I would have assumed him an accomplice and potential bargaining chip, not to mention keeping the professor here has the bonus effect of keeping him from retrieving help. In this, Nikolai's instincts are correct—at this point, a *mussor* patrol would only complicate matters for both of us.

"I thought you were on the run," Nikolai says. "Finding you in Aurestapol was a surprise. I almost didn't recognize you."

"I'm full of surprises."

"You're full of something, but I'm not sure it's surprises." The corner of Nikolai's mouth twitches. I think it's supposed to be a wry smile, but it's little more than mock bravado. He isn't wearing the glove on his right hand, and his knuckles are white from gripping the handle of his FP. The fingers and back of his hand are covered with bright red splotches, like a mild case of psoriasis.

"What is...what is all this, Mr. Titov?" Voynov stammers.

"I'm sorry about this, professor," I say. The dead face of the woman on the snowy road flashes through my mind, curdling my stomach. I can't let that happen to the professor.

Yet, if I allow myself to be captured, I have no idea about my fate. I don't know who I can trust in The Order anymore, but something tells me that Nikolai isn't one of them. That said, I don't get the feeling that any of this is personal on his part. Nikolai stumbled across me, recognized me from some briefing perhaps, and is trying to do what he thinks is right. At least that's my new hope.

"I'm not a traitor or a criminal or even on the run," I say.

"It's all a misunderstanding, I assume," Nikolai says.

I wish that were true, but this is more sinister than a simple misunderstanding. I've come to terms with Katalin Kovac being part of The Order, but then that means The Order wants to do me ill, even if I'm not completely sure what that ill is. Or at least whoever Katalin Kovac is in league with in The Order wants bad things for me. I don't know who Nikolai is aligned with, so I must assume the worst.

"A misunderstanding of sorts," I say.

"Professor Voynov is it? What is your business with...Mr. Titov?"

"I don't know who this man is," Voynov says. His voice quivers with fear. "He found me—"

"Professor, please—" But my attempted interruption doesn't work.

"—and had some questions about some sand."

"Sand?" asks Nikolai.

"Sand, yes. Sand. But I am an agronomist, you see. I know about soil, not sand. I study soil fertility."

I wish Voynov would shut up, but I realize that short of killing him, there is no way to ensure his

silence; why wouldn't he cooperate, especially when
threatened with the wrong end of a FP? He has no
special loyalty to me. He also has no malicious intent.
Voynov strikes me as a loyal citizen of the Empire, so
I can't hold any malice against him. Besides, while
what he knows would be better for me if left unsaid,
nothing he knows is particularly fatal to my cause.
Voynov knows little about the sand—where I got it,
what I went through to get it, and therefore, what it
means to me.

It takes Nikolai several tries to regain control of
the conversation, but he finally gets the professor to
stop babbling about his research interests.

"Where is this sand you speak of?" Nikolai asks.

"I was just looking for it," Voynov says.

"It's somewhere in this mess," I say. When I start
to turn back to the bench as if to search for the phial,
Nikolai jabs his FP in my direction.

"Not you." He motions me aside with a wave of
his pistol.

I step away, toward the side of the work bench
where the Kjeldahl apparatus bubbles away.

Nikolai releases Voynov's collar and nudges him
forward. "Find it and give it to me."

Voynov straightens his shirt and sheepishly starts
to search the workbench again.

As I had hoped, Nikolai is forced to split his
attention between the professor and me. Nikolai also
no longer seems to care that my hands are down. I
lowered them when I turned to search the
workbench, and he never ordered me to put them
back up. I make no moves that will draw attention to
this. I pretend to watch Voynov search the
workbench, and even wear a concerned expression,

which seems to increase Nikolai's desire to get the phial of sand.

"Hurry up," he says.

"I can't find it." Voynov is sweating heavily as he searches under the same notebook for the third time. Scared, he's not able to function in any sort of logical, systematic way—exactly how I would expect a civilian to respond.

Nikolai's patience is wearing thin. Less of his attention is focused on me now. The tip of his FP dips a little.

I shift my body slightly to hide my hand coming up to the top of the workbench. My fingers creep toward the alcohol burner. The glass reservoir is about the size of my fist and nearly full of fuel. It looks sturdy, and I doubt it will break unless I smash it on the floor, but getting hit by it would hurt, and if luck is with me, might even knock out Nikolai. If nothing, it'll give me a chance to get inside his weapon where I'll at least have a chance in a fight.

Nikolai notices me, only too late. "What are—"

I swing my arm around while stepping to the side, and fling the alcohol burner at Nikolai. His FP stutters and the neck of the bubbling glass flask shatters as fletchettes whistle through the spot where I was standing a half second ago. Nikolai tries to duck my throw, but the burner hits him in the side of the head, opening a jagged gash near his right temple. He recoils away, his weapon discharging wildly.

Voynov screams as fletchettes thunk into the wooden window frame and bench top. Stumbling away, Voynov falls, pulling some of the workbench clutter onto him.

I grab the metal work stand that was holding the

now broken flask over the alcohol burner. As I swing it, the flask is sent flying. It shatters against the far wall, splatter boiling liquid that sizzles on the plaster. As the stand comes around, its base cracks against the inside of Nikolai's right wrist. His FP flies from his grip and crashes through the glassware on the shelves next to the doorway and bounces to the floor in the professor's office.

I strike out with my boot at Nikolai's knee, but he manages to turn enough so that my attack glances off his left leg. He throws himself at me and we crash against the workbench, knocking over the rest of the Kjeldahl apparatus. The condenser column shatters, spraying water and broken glass onto the bench top and floor. Nikolai lands several punches into my side, but wrapped up as we are, he can't get much power behind them. I try to throw him aside, but bent backward over the bench as I am, I can't get the leverage I need, so I wrap my fingers through his hair and pull back his head.

His glasses have been dislodged, and blood smears the right side of his face from the cut opened by the alcohol burner.

Nikolai grimaces. He punches me again, this time catching my lowest rib.

I let out a surprised grunt, and he strikes the same rib a second time. His oiled hair slips through my grip.

He wraps his arms around my waist and picks me up. Off balance, we both tumble into the shelves of glassware, ripping them from the wall. The sound of breaking glass is thunderous. Surely everyone in the building can hear our fight.

I'm slammed down onto the bench top. The glass

shards cut into my shoulder. The air is nearly knocked from lungs, and I struggle to catch my breath. I cough, tasting smoke.

Out the corner of my eye, I see the grayed sheet covering the doorway has caught fire from the alcohol burner on the floor and the stacks of old journals and research notes on the workbench are smoldering.

Nikoklai uses his weight to keep me pinned atop the workbench. He shakes me a few times, trying to knock my head against its wooden surface, but I absorb the blows with my shoulders. His breathing comes in heavy bursts as he starts to tire. His grip on my arm weakens enough that I can shake my left fist free, and I land a solid blow to his jaw that staggers him.

The knuckles on my middle fingers pop painfully, and I withdraw my hand protectively to my chest. Sparks flare in my vision as pain shoots up to my elbow.

Nikolai stumbles away from me. Flames leap up as the papers on workbench catch fire. I barely manage to roll away before they do. The fire spreads rapidly as chemicals from some of the broken bottles catch. Green smoke mingles with the gray smoke already filling the upper half of the room. My eyes sting, and it is nearly impossible to draw a full breath.

The plaster wall above the lintel is now burning, and the door frame smokes heavily.

Nikolai recovers and drops into a defensive crouch in the middle of the lab. He is framed by the splattered red liquid as it hisses and smolders on the wall behind him. He stares at me, panting as smoke swirls down from the ceiling.

Professor Voynov sits on the floor with his back to the workbench, looking dazed. He cradles his right arm in his lap as blood drips from his fingertips.

Nikolai's gaze shoots from me to the rapidly spreading fire. He feints in my direction, then covers his head and leaps through the flames into Voynov's office. I'm about to follow Nikolai, but the professor coughs weakly.

Nikolai will get away, but even though I want to pursue him, he doesn't matter anymore. If I do not get Voynov out here, he will die, and I cannot allow that to happen.

"Get up!" I tug at the shoulder of the professor's jacket. He stares blankly up at me. The knuckles on my left hand have swelled so that I can barely move the fingers, but I still manage to pull Voynov to his feet. I squeeze his bearded chin in my right hand and wrench his face toward mine so I can stare directly into his eyes. "We have to go," I say, enunciating every word slowly and clearly so he can hear me over the growing roar of the flames.

Much as Nikolai leaped through the flames, Voynov and I can do the same, but it will take both of us if we're to succeed.

Voynov blinks several times as he seems to shake off his mental malaise.

My stomach turns suddenly, as if I've been dropped from the roof of a building. The smoke freezes in mid-swirl and the speed at which Voynov's eyes widen and mouth opens slows to a crawl. Everything—smoke and ash, flickering flames, the droplets of blood—stutters to stop.

I've learned through experience to never hesitate when my Talent speaks because that brief moment may be all I have to save my life.

I throw myself against Voynov, shielding him from the fire, and raise my left arm to cover my head as time leaps forward again. The flames flare up, fueled by a bursting chemical bottle. The hairs on the back of my left hand singe and the skin bubbles on my already swollen knuckles. Flaming splinters of glass pepper my back like buckshot, but my long coat turns them aside.

The fire is everywhere now, and the smoke so thick I can't see the doorway anymore. The room is a furnace, and I pull my smoldering long coat up to shield my head from the heat. I don't dare draw a breath, or risk singeing my throat and lungs. Tears stream down my face; I can barely keep my eyes open they sting so much.

As I stumble back from the flames, my foot brushes against the metal work stand lying on the floor. I grab the hot metal and swing it at the window shattering the glass. Air and smoke hiss out. The flames roar with even greater intensity as if fed by a giant pumping a monstrous bellows. I drag the base of the work stand around the window frame, clearing the jagged pieces of glass.

I grip the edge of the counter as my head spins. Any second the smoke and heat will overcome me, but I cannot leave the professor behind. I push Voynov toward the window, and he claws his way towards the clean air. When he hesitates at the opening, I shove him forcefully, and with a surprised yelp, he tumbles out of sight.

I follow him, cutting myself in several places as I slither through the broken glass and fall heavily into shrubbery next to Voynov. I roll over, violently coughing smoke from my lungs.

Next to me, Voynov wheezes and sputters. His face is blackened with soot, his beard peppered with ash. He looks over at me. "I'm alive," he says hoarsely. "Thank you."

A wail grows in pitch as someone cranks up the university's emergency siren.

Thick smoke billows out the window above us; otherwise the fire is contained for now by the stone wall. I touch my trouser pocket, and I'm relieved to feel the phial is still intact. "Come on."

We crawl through the bushes to the lawn where Voynov collapses. Coughs wrack his body as he struggles to clear the smoke from his lungs.

"Stay here. I'll get help."

On the stairs of the building, faculty members frantically direct students from the atrium out onto the lawn. Many others stare in dazed clusters at the smoke now streaming from multiple windows. A panicked cry erupts when the first orange flames lick out from Voynov's. I see no sign of Nikolai, but I'm sure he escaped the fire.

Three young men run across the lawn toward me, and I reflexively drop into a defensive posture.

"Are you okay?" the first student asks as he nears.

I lower my fists. "I'm okay, but Professor Voynov needs help."

The three students drop their satchels of books and rush past me. They duck back momentarily as flames blast out from Voynov's window before being sucked back inside; then they rush in low to the professor. Slinging his arms over their shoulders, two of them pull Voynov to his feet while the third reassures him.

Voynov is in safe hands, so I slip away across the lawn, and melt through the growing crowd.

My heart is still pounding when I reach the edge of campus, but only then do I take a second to see if I am being followed. From the direction of the science building, a column of smoke rises over the trees, where it mingles with the thick cloud pack. The clang of a fire tank fills the gloom. People—students mostly, but others, too—rush by me toward the fire. Good people, rushing toward signs of danger to help. These are the soul of this great Empire.

Guilt knots my innards as I move against them. I wish I could do more, but I need to get as far away from here as possible. Likely Nikolai has gone for help, and I expect Aurestapol will be a very dangerous place for me by nightfall—even more so than it already is. I should head straight for Grand Station and get on the first train to anywhere, but as always seems to be my lot, I have one more thing I must do in this city.

No one appears to be paying me any attention so I snap up the collar of my coat with my right hand. The left throbs as I flex its fingers. The knuckles are swollen and burned, but I don't think anything is broken. Inside my coat, I take the handle of my FP, but my grip is weak, and I doubt I can steady the weapon sufficiently to shoot it accurately. I transfer my FP from its left-draw shoulder holster to the right pocket of my long coat. I haven't used my offhand since my initial training, but at that time I was an adequate shot with it. That was a long time ago, however.

I head off campus into the avenues of Aurestapol then double back several times, change my pace, and

criss-cross the streets to confirm no one is tailing me.
Satisfied, I turn toward St. Vladimir's Church. Birdie
won't be there yet, but I have nowhere else to go that
I am certain is safe. Given my situation, Birdie would
understand if I chose to skip our rendezvous, yet
something in my gut tells me not to leave without
speaking with her. Besides, and more importantly, I
need to get her to deliver a warning to Lera.

Nikolai now knows her connection to me extends
beyond my role in delivering her to The Order. What
he will do with that information, I do not know—too
many variables go into that prediction—and that
uncertainty causes me considerable consternation.
Will Nikolai pass the information up the chain? Will
Katalin Kovac or any of her associates learn of it?
And what will they do?

I have selfishly put Lera into needless danger.

I spit curses under my breath as I arrive at my
destination.

The perimeter boxwood hedge, green even this
late in the winter, hides the park's stone tables and
benches from the streets. During better times, these
tables hosted old men playing chess and dominoes,
but war and winter have left the park empty and
bleak. I sit and wait in the shadow of a statue of
Gabriel, the child saint of Białystok. The weathered
marble is a dingy brown, and a crown of rotting
leaves is plastered to its head.

As a child at the orphanage, Mistress Markov made
me pray to St. Gabriel. He was our patron, she would
remind us at every opportunity, saying his grace
protected us all. I never felt particularly safe under his
protection, but now, staring up into his statue's
marble eyes, I pray that his grace keeps Lera safe.

The hours slide by, the day grows colder, the clouds thicker, and my coat isn't enough to keep the chill out indefinitely. Even a few swigs of vodka from Krauss's flask cannot keep the cold from settling into my bones. My left hand throbs. The knuckles have turned purple, and much of the back of my hand has swelled such that the skin is hot and tight. I may have broken a knuckle after all.

By the time Birdie's shoe click on the stone path, I'm shivering and glum.

Birdie peels back her hood. Her blond hair and ice blue eyes shine in the strangely desaturated light. She doesn't hide her surprise as I rise from the bench to greet her.

"What happened to you?" With her thumb, she wipes a smudge of ash from the side of my face. "On second thought, I don't want to know."

Good. If I start to speak, I fear my teeth will start chattering. It's all I can do to squeeze out a single intelligible word. "Anything?"

"Nothing on the whereabouts of your friend," Birdie says. "Sorry."

I didn't have a lot of hope she would hear much, and if she did, I had even less hope it would be good news. I'm confident Gorelov is out of my reach by now, either on the run out of Aurestapol, or in the hands of Red Cuffs, or dead. The best I could have hoped from Birdie would have been learning which of these was true.

"But..."

Birdie suddenly has my attention again.

"...I heard some things about your friend of which I don't know what to make. He doesn't have much presence in the rumor space, but what little is out there links him to something called Room Twenty-two."

My brow pinches together.

"I've never heard of it, either," Birdie says, noticing my puzzlement, "so I listened around, and it has an even lower profile than your Mr. Gorleov. The only thing I heard is this Room Twenty-two seems to be linked to Motoska."

"As in Motoska Island? The prison?"

Birdie shrugs. "I thought you said he worked for the Ministry of Ethics and Culture."

"That's what I thought." My feet tingle painfully as I pace in front to the statue trying to get my blood flowing again. Motoska Island is the Empire's most notorious prison. If you believe the stories, it is reserved for the vilest, most dangerous, criminals in the Empire—men so evil that killing them is to deny justice to their victims—so they are locked away in tiny cages, locked inside cells, locked inside wards, locked behind great gates on an island shrouded in the mists, surrounded by raging rapids, and reachable only by dirigible. Those stories are ludicrous beyond reason, and likely only myths created to scare people, but that doesn't make a link to the Empire's most notorious prison any less perplexing.

"Maybe he's not with the Ministry of Ethics and Culture," I say.

"You think? But that's only one of the strange bits," she says.

"There's more?" I'm feeling much warmer now, as much a product of my activity as Birdie's intrigue.

I'm the only one here, but still she lowers her voice. "A while ago I started hearing chatter about a place called Aksaray, in the Sultanate. Something about an archeological dig, but nothing particularly compelling—Class C stuff that barely gets my ears tingling these days. The sources were scholarly, not military—"

"Why is this relevant?" I ask.

Birdie's lips press together, annoyed at my interruption. "Everything I hear is relevant, even if I don't see the immediate connection. That's the way it works."

I'm not buying it, but I don't say anything. I haven't a clue how anyone's Talent works, but if Birdie says it is relevant to her, then great. This doesn't sound relevant to *me*.

"As I was saying," Birdie continues. "I first heard about Aksaray when I was listening around for news about our friend Olstevski. It didn't make any sense then, so I just filed it away. Sort of forgot about it."

"It's probably just a treasure hunt." It's no secret that Sultan Mehkmed has been selling off his land's historical artifacts to raise money. The Sultanate produces few exportable commodities; instead, it is a crossroads for goods moving from Quin and The Empire to western markets. The war has thrown those markets into turmoil, and reduced tariff revenues for the Sultanate.

But then Birdie says something that does catch my interest.

"Treasure hunt is what I thought at first, too, until this afternoon, when I heard Military Intelligence dispatched a man to Aksaray."

"That *is* interesting," I say, "but, not to be a cad, what has this got to do with me?"

"Again, I don't know, but I've been working your Gorelov problem exclusively today, and this is something that came to me. This tells me Aksaray is linked to Olstevski and Gorelov, or it's linked to you."

I consider Birdie's words. I have no reason to believe she's being untruthful with me. If she says this Aksaray news is linked to Olstevski, Gorelov, or, in some way, me, then I would be foolish to ignore her. "Do you know anything else?"

"Best I can piece together this is related to an archeological dig overseen by someone named Argola or Irogulu or something like that. He's a university type from Çavuş."

"Çavuş?"

"You know it."

I shrug. "Only by name. Did you learn anything else?"

"No. So, what's next?"

A good question. Gorelov seems to have disappeared entirely, and I still doubt I could get to Ordinburg in time to find his family. Either Gorelov has succeeded in getting a message to them, and they are safely away, or he hasn't, and they are in the hands of the Red Cuffs. Room Twenty-two? Even if there is an obvious path forward on that lead, I don't even want to think about anything linked to Motoska Island. That leaves the Aksaray dig. It sounds the least important of the things Birdie has shared, but it also happens to be in the same general area of one Dr. Arif Özel, the only person who might be able to help me learn something about the sand in my pocket.

Birdie watches me uncertainly as I pace the stones in front of the statue of St. Gabriel, weighing this overload of information. My decision made, I stop pacing.

"You've already done a lot," I say.

"We're in this together, remember?"

I give her a weak grin in acknowledgement. "Aurestapol has become too dangerous for me," I say. "It would be best for me leave immediately, but there are some things I have left undone." I fish a key out of my pocket. "Don't ask me to explain, but there's a person tied up in this flat."

Birdie sighs in exasperation and motions for me to give her the key. "What do I need to do?"

I drop the key into her outstretched hand and tell her the address. I then fish a coin out of my pocket and give that to her. "Hire a willing stranger to release the person, and by all means, make sure you aren't seen and you can't be identified."

Birdie frowns in displeasure, but the key and the coin disappear under her cloak. "Are you going to tell me who it is? We're in this together, *remember*?"

She's right to call me on it—old habits and all. "His name is Mélon. He's one of us."

Birdie's eyebrows rise. "The Order," she whispers.

"He was my initial contact in Coruşu, the one who set everything up. Katalin Kovac is his handler."

Birdie's surprised expression narrows into something more dangerous. "You want to just let him go? That's mighty charitable of you."

"I don't know his true role in this, so I'm not ready to cross any lines."

Birdie nods, but her pursed lips tell me she doesn't agree.

"I have one more ask," I say, my gaze dropping to the ground. "It's Lera."

"You didn't go find her."

"I know, bad move, but I needed to thank her for

what the two of you did for me Coruşu.
Unfortunately, an agent named Nikolai saw us talking.
I learned later that he recognized me."

Birdie shakes her head disapprovingly. "I take it
he's still alive, too? Hmph. That's going to cause her
some trouble."

"The only question is how much. I need you to
warn her, and—"

"There's more?"

"Keep an eye on her."

A grin spreads across Birdie's face. "You're
worried about her."

"She's just a kid."

Birdie's grin broadens. "I'll do what I can, but you
owe me. What are you going to do now?"

"After all this, I need another holiday. I was
thinking some place warm this time. Some place
where I can find some good *raki*."

And, I hope, some answers.

End of Book Three

Thank you for reading Book Three of the Calypto
Cycle. Gaining exposure as an independent author
relies mostly on word-of-mouth, so if you have the
time and inclination, please consider leaving a short
review wherever you can.

MEET THE AUTHOR

D. Thomas Minton writes from his home in the Pacific Northwest of the United States, where he lives a short walk from vineyards and alpaca farms. When not writing, he travels to remote locations and helps communities across the Pacific Ocean protect coral reefs. His stories have appeared in some of science fiction's top publications. He can found online at dthomasminton.com.

A sneak peek at
Messages from the Sand
Book Four of the Calypto Cycle

AHMET'S THICK BLACK MOUSTACHE quivers as he glares down at me from his perch atop a dusty rock at the edge of the work area. He is Dr. Eroğlu's foreman who oversees the foreign diggers, and he's never tried to hide his disdain for us.

Too spent to care, I lean against the shaft of my shovel trying to catch my breath in the thin air. Two weeks on the flanks of *Hasan daği* has yet to thicken my blood enough for the hard labor into which I have indentured myself.

Ahmet curses me in Turkic, punctuating each word with a sharp snap of a slender switch against his left palm. To my knowledge, he has never used the switch on anyone, and I suspect he would never actually strike one of the foreign crew. Dr. Eroğlu can't afford to lose any of us due to mistreatment.

Ahmet jumps down from his rock, kicking up a cloud of fine ochre dust. The hem of his *jubba* is yellow from the dirt. "Dr. Eroğlu wants this rubble cleared this afternoon," he says, glaring at me, but speaking to the diggers.

The plink of the pickaxes increases. Today we are reducing the hardpan in the northern corner of the excavated building to siftable-sized rubble. Yunus, one of Dr. Eroğlu's students, coordinates our labor to

165

ensure we don't "disrupt the context" of any artifacts we might uncover.

Jonathan grins at me as he muscles past with a wheelbarrow full of head-sized stones. "Dig, Mahmoud bey." His Turkic is respectable, but his accent betrays his Angliyan heritage. Jonathan arrived at the Aksaray worksite a month ago, along with a handful of other diggers from all corners of the world. Since then, foreign help has continued to trickle in, which allowed me to join Dr. Eroğlu's crew without raising any suspicions.

I straighten, flexing the fingers of my left hand. The knuckle I injured in my fight with Nikolai in Aurestapol last month has taken to aching again. I thought it fully healed after my week-long transit from the small port at Maruipol to Samsun in the Sultanate, and then up into the Aksaray highlands, but the intense manual labor has proven otherwise. Shoveling is painful, but less so than swinging a pickaxe.

Jonathan returns with an empty wheelbarrow and parks it next to me. He loosens the ends of his *keffiyeh* from under his chin and lets the checkered cloth hang down the left side of his face.

I dump a half-shovel of fist-sized rocks into it, then I let the shovel's shaft linger on the wheelbarrow's edge while I draw two breaths. The air tastes of metal, and the fine dust that coats my tongue gets into everything: the food, the water barrels, my blanket, the folds of my ears.

"I don't see the hurry," Jonathan says just loud enough to be heard over the rattle of metal sieves to our left.

"Hurry and wait," I say, conscious of my accent. I

have told everyone my name is Mahmoud, from El
Emir. My physical appearance is sufficient to carry
this ruse, but I must watch my pronunciations so as
not to betray my true Empirical heritage. I have
spent enough time in in El Emir—time I have often
wanted to forget—that I am familiar with their
inflections and habits well enough to fool all but the
most astute.

To my left, Ramón grumbles as he hefts his pick
and buries the point a hands width into the ground.
"Dig or stand, coin is coin, all the same." His accent
is thick enough that it barely sounds like Turkic.
"Might as well be useful."

Ramón says he's a displaced iron worker from the
southern coast of Ispaniya, but that story is no less a
fable than mine. The only difference is Ramón lacks
the skill to execute his ruse. He is from Empire -- his
real name is Mikhail or Petr or something similar, it
does not matter. Given the clumsiness of his craft, I
also have little doubt he is the military intelligence
officer Birdie mentioned at our last meeting in
Aurestapol. The military may stamp out efficient
killers, but they craft lousy spies.

The swipe of Jonathan's forearm across his brow
hides the roll of his eyes. Ramón's comically poor
Ispaniyan accent does not even fool him.

"Standing is less wear on the body," I say with a
half-hearted chuckle as the knuckles on my left hand
continue to ache. While Jonathan and the other
foreign nationals have taken to shunning our fake
Ispaniyan, I have tried to keep an amicable
relationship in order to learn what he might know.
I'm not here out of any academic interest in history or
on a mission from The Order, the organization who

until a short while ago was my life. Three weeks ago, Birdie told me this dig was somehow linked to my recent misfortunes, but she couldn't tell me anything more than that. I believe her, however, because she has a Talent for hearing pertinent things, improbable as that may sound. I don't pretend to understand it, just as I don't pretend to understand how my Talent works. It just does.

Look for
Messages from the Sand, Book Four of the Calypto Cycle at an online vendor near you in 2018.